She said,
She said

She said, She said

Celeste O. Norfleet & Jennifer Norfleet

KIMANI
tru
™

SHE SAID, SHE SAID

ISBN-13: 978-0-373-83091-6
ISBN-10:   0-373-83091-2

www.KimaniTRU.com

Printed in U.S.A.

To Fate & Fortune

Acknowledgment

I would like to thank and acknowledge my coauthor Jennifer Norfleet. You're a wonderful daughter and teacher. I learned so much about myself as a writer and as a mother. Writing with you at my side was an experience that I will always treasure. I'd also like to thank Christopher for giving me additional insight into teen life. And, as always, a special thanks to Charles.

Celeste

I would like 2 thank my mom, Celeste O. Norfleet 4 putting up with me through this whole process, and 4 helping me learn more about writing. I'd also like 2 thank my 5 BFFs, U all kno who U R!

Jennifer =]

Special thanks to Linda Gill and Evette Porter for giving us the opportunity to go on this incredible journey together. Also special thanks to Elaine English for your constant support and direction.

We'd also like to thank our family and friends for putting up with our craziness throughout this process. Your prayers and well wishes were a blessing and greatly appreciated.

Please send your comments to conorfleet@aol.com, jenniferrr54@yahoo.com or Celeste O. Norfleet/ Jennifer Norfleet, P.O. Box 7346, Woodbridge, VA 22195-7346.

chapter 1

Tamika

Tamika Fraser felt like screaming.

The words, already permanently etched in her mind, scrambled and unscrambled as she shook her head in disbelief. This wasn't happening. It was the last thing she expected, the last thing she had imagined. This just couldn't be happening. She read the note again. Yep, for real, it was happening.

Still in shock, she crumpled and tossed the neatly scripted phone message her mother had just given her across the room, aiming for the trash can in the corner. Usually it was an easy shot for her, but today she missed. She should have seen the handwriting on the wall. Nothing was going to be as it should. Not today.

Her mother, Laura, reached down and picked up the crumpled note and dropped it into the trash can. "Tamika, getting upset isn't going to change anything and there's no sense sulking and pouting. There's nothing you can do about it right now, so why don't you…"

Blah, blah, blah. That's all Tamika heard as she sat there

not listening to her mother continue with her happy-land speech about life lessons. Always positive and always optimistic, Laura Fraser was as usual completely clueless. She had no idea what it felt like to be disappointed or to want something so badly and have it inches from your fingertips, then have it ripped away. How could she? Her life was always and forever perfect.

"…after all, it's just two weeks…"

Yeah, right, just two weeks. Tamika shook her head. Two weeks was a lifetime as far as she was concerned. It might as well be two months.

Why was this happening to her? She'd done everything right, hadn't she? Of course she had. This was too important to her and for the past two months she had lived, breathed and dreamt about the Massachusetts Regional Photo Camp Internship program.

It was the first of its kind, sponsored by a well-known photographer. It was a workshop on photography that was a for-real stepping stone to her future as a photojournalist. She had paid for it with her own money.

In preparation she had even quit her job at the mall so that she would have plenty of time to participate. The internship was a major event and having been selected to participate was an honor. Under the guidance of a half-dozen recognized photographers, she was eager and excited to attend.

The possibility of being taught by a professional in her chosen field was major. And the final coup was the contest with a grand prize of having the winner's photo published in a national magazine. But because of a mix-up, the internship she'd planned to start in two days had been postponed for two weeks. That meant sitting around the house waiting.

"...to tell you the truth I had a few questions about that camp anyway. Maybe you should have—"

"Mom, we talked about this already."

"Yes, I know, but tell me, how much do you really know about this program? I mean, it's not even listed as a formal accredited class in the college curriculum and the class location sites they suggested are extremely questionable to say the least, including the one that requires you to be out half the night."

"It's sponsored by an alumnus of the University of Massachusetts and it's an incredible opportunity. Do you know what this could do for my college application? Not to mention the possibility of having my work seen and critiqued by professionals. I could even have my work appear in a major magazine."

"Why don't you look for something more suited to your—"

"Mom, please, okay?" Tamika said.

"Fine, fine. Whatever. Just get ready for dinner. It's almost ready," Laura said, ending the topic of conversation. Tamika watched as she sighed heavily, walked to the door then paused to take one last look around the room.

"Is that it?" Tamika asked.

"So, how was your last day of school?"

"A'ight, I guess," Tamika said, not wanting to get into another serious discussion.

"That's it, just all right? You're in eleventh grade now, just two more years until college. It's that exciting?"

Tamika shrugged. "I guess."

Laura forced a smile. "Well, I think it's exciting. But I still can't believe that you're going to college so soon."

"I still have two more years, Mom, remember?"

"I didn't mean to make it sound like I'm trying to get rid of you. I just want you to realize that time is moving fast. Two years will fly by in a flash. I know the first sixteen did." Tamika nodded. "So, how's Lisa doing? Is she ready for the big move to California?"

"She's fine. She's getting ready," Tamika said as Laura nodded. "Is that it?" Tamika repeated, hoping to hasten her mother's departure so that she could be alone again.

"Yes, just come on down for dinner, okay?"

"A'ight, I'll be right there."

Her mother left.

Finally. Tamika flopped back onto the bed and stared up at the ceiling. Crap, now what? She blew out exasperatedly.

Being too young to work last year was the worst. Her father had gone on a two-month-long business trip and she was stuck home with her mother. The only relief was when her dad came home. But then they separated for a while, like three weeks. Then they got back together, but that's a whole 'nother story. They thought she didn't know why they separated, but she did.

This year she'd planned ahead; at least she thought she had. She glanced at the trash can.

After hanging out at the mall all afternoon with her best friend, Lisa, Tamika felt herself getting stressed all over again. It was the last day of school, but unlike most sixteen-year-olds, she didn't mind going to school. It was being home that was nerve-racking. At school—for those six and a half hours—she was perfect, popular, confident. But at home all that disappeared. There was no way she could compare with her mother, "Laura the Perfectly Flawless."

Now the numbness of being stuck in the house for another two weeks had drama written all over it. Since her mother's layoff six months ago and not finding another job or anything else to occupy her time, her main occupation had become driving Tamika crazy. She was good at it. But at least it was only two days since she was leaving soon. She was going away for a whole month to go back to her hometown to take care of some family business.

Tamika smiled—a whole month without her mother. At least something was still going right. Of course, her father would be there, but he was always so into his work that he rarely glanced up long enough to see what she was up to.

She got up off the bed and headed to the open door, then turned when she heard her cell phone buzzing on the nightstand. She had a text message.

Lisa: \(^_^)
Tamika: (^_^)/
Lisa: wassup?
Tamika: noth-N -U
Lisa: jst chill-N
Tamika: what R U doing?
Lisa: packin
Tamika: I still can't beliv U'R movin
Lisa: I know—weird

"Tamika, come on. Dinner's almost ready."

Tamika moaned and rolled her eyes. The last thing she wanted to deal with was another one of her mother's perfect dinners, candles, tablecloth, good china, the whole nine yards. Seriously, she had no idea why her mother had to celebrate every occasion as if it were the dawn of time or something. Birthdays, her anniversary, every meaningless holiday on the calendar, a good report card, when somebody coughed, when she dropped a pencil, when she picked it up. They were all superspecial occasions as far as her mother was concerned. But going out to celebrate was totally out of the question.

But that came with being perfect. Everything had to be neat and perfect too. It was Laura Hopkins Fraser's rule, probably passed on from mother to daughter. Tamika smirked. Pity. The gene had evidently been passed down from generation to generation, but from a quick look at her bedroom, it was obvious that the gene had skipped her.

Not bothering to answer, Tamika continued texting her friend.

Tamika: really weird
Lisa: can u beliv skool is ovr?
Tamika: yeah :)
Lisa: finally—11th grade :)
Tamika: 2 more yrs 2 freedom
Lisa: heard that
Tamika: R U stil going 2nite?
Lisa: yeah—U
Tamika: definitely
Lisa: wht R U wearin?

"Tamika!"

"Comin'," she hollered and went right back to what she was doing, knowing she had plenty of time.

Tamika: WhT h%die, jeans and Vans—U?
Lisa: Ditto—GrN h%die
Tamika: I saw Drea & Lexea 2day
Lisa: Ewww
Tamika: I know

Lisa: they speak 2 U
Tamika: hell no
Lisa: LOL—heard that
Tamika: talkin 2 Justin
Lisa: OMG—Ouch:-O
Tamika: I know
Lisa: Wht happened?
Tamika: I went off
Lisa: 4real LOL!
Tamika: He wants time
Lisa: 4 wht?
Tamika: !?! Hater
Lisa: U 2 break up?

Tamika paused to consider her answer. She started to text her response but then deleted it and retyped a single word.

Tamika: Maybe
Lisa: ?

"Tamika, did you hear me? Let's go, now."

"I hear you so stop screaming my name. Jeez," Tamika muttered to herself. "I'm coming now, Mom," she said, answering aloud, then resumed texting on her cell phone.

Tamika: Grrr!
Lisa: Wht?
Tamika: My mom *@* %!
Lisa: LOL!
Lisa: When is she leavin?
Tamika: N 2 days—can't wait
Lisa: I bet

Tamika: No mom drama 4 A month
Lisa: U'R dad?
Tamika: will B @ work all day
Lisa: :)
Tamika: I know right
Lisa: LOL!
Tamika: LOL!

Tamika's ring tone sounded. She told Lisa to hold up a second and clicked over to answer. "Hello."

"Are you coming down to dinner sometime soon or would you prefer that I hire a servant and have him bring your dinner up to you on a silver platter?" her mother said sarcastically.

Tamika's first impulse was to get smart and choose the silver tray, but she decided against it. "Yes, Mom. I heard you. I'm coming down," she said, then walked over to her bathroom. "I'm in the bathroom," she added truthfully, standing in the open doorway.

"Fine, wash your hands and come on down."

Tamika clicked off. Oddly enough she was slightly impressed that her mother had enough ingenuity to call her cell. She clicked back to Lisa.

Lisa: R U there?
Tamika: I G2G
Lisa: K
Tamika: CUL8R
Lisa: 1G%dThg-NoMoreskool!
Lisa/Tamika: \(^_^)/!

"Coming." Tamika closed her cell and put it in the back pocket of her jeans. The text conversation with her best friend, Lisa Carter, always made her feel better, even if they hadn't actually talked.

Lisa lived down the street and even though they talked in school all day, had lunch together and then talked on the bus ride home, they still texted each other constantly.

Inseparable, they'd been best friends since grade school even though they were total opposites. Tamika was thin, athletic and outgoing. Lisa was studious and slightly over-weight. They complemented each other perfectly and did everything together. When Tamika got braces Lisa did too. When Lisa got her hair relaxed and had to cut it because it was damaged, Tamika cut her hair too. Best friends for life, they even planned on attending the same college and one day opening a business together. Of course, they had no idea what it would be, but neither cared as long as they were still friends.

When her parents divorced and her mother moved to California, Lisa was devastated but Tamika was right there by her side. That's what friends did: they supported each other no matter what. Now that Lisa was going out to California to live with her mother, they were both bummed. Even thinking about it was hard. How was she going to attend Hayden High without Lisa?

Well, Lisa was right about one thing—no more school. And since she made a complete and total fool of herself, she needed a nice long break. What was she thinking walking up to Justin acting all jealous? It's not as if he was actually interested in Drea or Lexea anyway.

Everybody knew they were skanks. And it wasn't as if she and Justin were all that tight anymore anyway. Their *thing* had chilled weeks ago.

"Tamika Fraser, let's go. What's taking so long?" The

voice shrieked again for the hundredth time in the last ten minutes. "Tamika, now."

"I'm coming," she answered, taking one last look at her reflection in the mirror hanging on the back of her door. She smiled. Her face had definitely cleared up after the last bout of acne she had had a few weeks ago. She added a touch of lip gloss and fluffed her hair, pleased with her appearance. She had decided to go natural about six months ago. A soft, blown-out Afro crowned her small face now. It was a bold statement and she loved it.

"Tamika, would you please get down here? Dinner is on the table now. Why do I have to call you seven or eight times?"

Tamika rolled her eyes. Her mother always asked ridiculous questions, knowing that the answer was not what she'd want to hear. Since a response was out of the question, why bother?

chapter 2

Laura

"Ugh, that child, I swear, she does this on purpose," Laura muttered as she walked back into the kitchen still agitated by her daughter, an everyday occurrence in the Fraser household. Laura knew that Tamika loved her, of course, but the two of them living together in the same house was damn near impossible. Two women under one roof was guaranteed drama, and they delivered daily.

Ever since Tamika turned thirteen she'd been impossible to live with. It was like adding the word *teen* to the end of her age somehow killed off a hundred or so brain cells. The once agreeable daughter she so adored was now an irritable, sullen, irresponsible shrew who hated everything and everyone, particularly when she didn't get her way, which was often.

Laura took a moment to consider the photo camp internship. She didn't like it even when her husband agreed, but she relented to keep the peace. At least now she had a legitimate reason for changing her mind.

"I swear that child is going to drive me crazy one of these days," she said aloud.

"Now what?"

Laura turned to see her husband standing in the open refrigerator with a carton of orange juice in his hand. "When did you get in?" she asked as she grabbed a glass and handed it to him.

"A few minutes ago. You two at it again?"

"Excuse me?"

"You and Tamika. I heard you calling her down."

"Dinner's almost ready and she's pissed as usual."

"Pissed off? Did you tell her already?"

"No," Laura said coolly. "There was a problem with her summer camp thing. There was a mix-up and it won't be starting for another two weeks."

"Oh, good, so you'll probably be back by then."

"What, in two weeks? Are you kidding me?"

"Come on, it'll probably only take just a few weeks, if that," he said.

"Do you have any idea how many years—hell, decades and centuries—are in that house?"

"Fine."

"No, not fine. That house goes back to my great-great-grandmother. There are things still in there from her generation and before."

"Well, maybe. Okay, fine," Malcolm Fraser said, no longer interested in talking about it.

Laura turned away without responding. He was also driving her crazy. Of all the times to do this to them again. She walked over to the roast and grabbed a carving knife and fork and began slicing the perfectly cooked beef. "I have no idea what I'm gonna do with her."

Malcolm, now sitting at the center island counter, chuckled to himself and just shook his head. "Don't get so stressed, Laura. She'll be down," he answered.

"It's not just that and you know it."

He opened his mouth, then quickly shut it. He probably figured that if he didn't respond they wouldn't discuss it again. Wrong.

"I have no idea what happened to us. We used to be..." Laura began, then stopped, holding back the flood of memories threatening to overwhelm her. "We used to be so close, we did everything together. I don't know what happened."

"She became a teenager," Malcolm said.

Laura stopped carving. She wasn't talking about Tamika, she was referring to her and her husband. But as usual he didn't have a clue, so she just let it pass. "That's a cop-out. She's still my daughter."

"And her life doesn't revolve around that fact anymore. But that's okay."

Laura let that statement pass too. She wasn't prepared to hear what he had to say. For the first time in her life she was losing control. Everything she had was falling apart and she was scared. Her thoughts swirled in circles constantly. Talking to someone would help. She glanced around, seeing her husband staring at his open laptop, engrossed as usual. Obviously he wasn't that someone.

"Okay, now seriously, Malcolm, can't somebody else do this thing?" she said, getting back to a previous conversation they'd started on the phone earlier.

"I told you, Laura, it's a great opportunity. It means that a promotion is right around the corner and it's only for a couple of months."

"A couple of months? You said one month," she said, turning to him still armed with the knife and fork.

Malcolm raised his arms jokingly in surrender, then walked over to her, smiling. "No, I said one month, maybe two. We won't know until we're actually on-site and see what that place looks like."

"We? We as in who else is going, Malcolm?" she asked with an accusatory tone in her voice.

"All right, let's not get back into that again."

"Oh, of course, let's not," she snapped sarcastically, then turned away from him.

"Laura, please, we talked about this. You have to learn to trust me again. What happened last year won't happen again, I promise you, I swear to you," he said, moving closer to her. "Laura…"

"Is she going?" Laura asked, putting the knife and fork down and turning around to see the expression on his face. She knew he couldn't hide the truth. Malcolm's affair with his coworker last year had eaten at her for months, and even though she'd said she put it behind her, every once in a while it crept back up to haunt them.

"Laura, you're right, I should have been honest with you when I first told you about this business trip. I'm not the only one going. There'll be four of us, me and—"

"No," she said, turning around quickly, "I don't want to know. You want me to trust you. Fine, fine, I'll trust you. Go, do what you have to do."

He smiled and reached out to her. "We can beat this thing, I know we can," he assured her.

She nodded, knowing that she might have forgiven him but she definitely hadn't forgotten what he'd done.

Malcolm smiled, as usual totally oblivious to her true emotions as he reached in and grabbed a tiny slice of meat, then popped it into his mouth. The perfectly roasted succulent meat dissolved instantly, trailing a seasoned sensation down his throat. "Umm, that's delicious," he added with a quick kiss on her cheek.

Laura nodded her head obligingly. She was getting so tired of all this. At thirty-nine years old she expected her life to be so different. She expected to have her own design company, to be married to a man who adored her and not his damn job and to have a daughter who was reasonably sane most of the time.

Instead she had just been laid off from a job she had had since a college internship, her husband had serious fidelity issues and her daughter was downright impossible to live with twenty-four hours a day, three hundred and sixty-five days a year. All this meant that her sanity constantly wavered somewhere between crazy and damn near neurotic.

"Now as for Tamika," Malcolm said, stealing another piece of meat, "she's a teenager and we're gonna get through that too."

"Yeah, I know," she said and watched as he popped another piece of meat into his mouth, then answered his buzzing phone. He walked into the adjoining room talking business as usual.

Laura picked up the knife and fork again and turned back to cutting the meat. Her husband's news was the last thing she needed and it couldn't have come at a worse time. After getting laid off six months ago she was still in shock. Then applying nonstop for a comparable position had only proved one thing for sure: she'd gotten old. Apparently no one wanted to hire a nearly forty-year-old advertising director or even a senior copywriter.

Then out of the blue last week she'd gotten a second interview with a very prestigious company. She was beyond thrilled. Unfortunately, earlier today she'd gotten a call that she didn't get the job. She called Malcolm in hopes of getting some empathy, but the call only added to her drama since he took the opportunity to inform her that he was leaving on a monthlong business trip.

So at this moment she was beyond stressed. She walked over to the window overlooking the small patch of yard and the bevy of plants. Her in-ground garden was green and lush, thanks to automatic sprinklers, but her potted flowers, pot-bound and strangling, drooped, stressed by the sur-roundings. They seemed to reflect her mood and she sympa-thized.

Laid off for who knows how long, she knew she needed a change. There was only so much grocery shopping, loads of laundry, vacuuming, dusting and mindless celebration planning a person could do without going insane. The opportunity to sell her parents' house had presented itself, and the idea to drive down was exactly what she needed and even more so now.

It was a change, a break, a much-needed time-out and some-thing that would hopefully prove that she was still alive. For the past month she'd been looking forward to going to her hometown alone. No responsibilities, no rules and no drama. Unfortunately now she'd be taking some of her drama with her.

"You and Tamika could use some mommy-and-me time."

"Some what?" she asked, looking at Malcolm as he returned to the kitchen area.

"Some mommy-and-me time. You know, together time to reconnect."

"Mommy and me?" Laura asked. "Honey, I don't know if you noticed it but our mommy-and-me days are long over."

"You know what I mean. The two of you could drive

down to Georgia together, stop at a few places along the way and make this into a really enjoyable road trip. By the time you get back we'll be ready to go to Martha's Vineyard for our usual two-week vacation. The summer will be over and you can decide about your career then."

Laura shrugged as she picked up and carried the salad bowl into the dining room and placed it on the table. She sighed. God, she hated it when he made sense and came up with good ideas. She slowly mulled over his suggestion as she neatened a place setting. Maybe he was right. Her original plan was to drive down, but since Malcolm had dropped his Tokyo bomb on her, driving hundreds of miles with a sulky teenager seemed like suicide. But maybe he was right. Maybe this was an opportunity to get closer to her daughter.

"Tamika," Laura called out again, then looked up, seeing her daughter finally coming downstairs. "There you are, finally. It's about time. When I call you, would you please do me the graciousness of at least answering me?"

"I did," Tamika said.

"I had to call your cell."

"See, and I answered," Tamika said. Laura glared at her. "I mean, I was busy but I was coming."

"So now I need to call your cell or text you in order to get your attention?" she asked rhetorically. Tamika smiled. Laura surmised that another meaningless circular conversation was about to begin. "Never mind, never mind, don't answer. I don't think I even want to know."

Tamika laughed.

Laura shook her head, half smiling at the absurdity. "Okay, fine. So, do you have any plans for this evening? If not, I thought we could go to the mall or something. Your dad probably has work to do so we can grab some ice cream and do some shopping maybe."

"Actually, I'm supposed to hang out with Lisa and some friends tonight."

"By some friends I presume you mean Justin," Laura said with obvious annoyance.

"Not necessarily, but yes, he'll be there," she said, knowing that her mother disliked him. "He's promoting it."

"Promoting it?" Laura asked.

"Okay, this is you being judgmental, right?"

"No, I'm not being judgmental. I just don't think you need to be so serious at your age. It's just too soon to get so attached. I didn't have a real boyfriend until I was well into college, definitely not in high school."

"We're not serious, we're just hangin'."

"Hanging as in boyfriend with perks?"

Tamika looked at her, astonished. "No, Mom, there are no perks. We're just hangin', that's all. No sex, okay? We've gone over this a million times."

"And we'll go over it a million more. Justin is not the kind of boy you need to be hanging around with. First of all, he's too old."

"He's a senior and I'm a junior."

"He's already eighteen years old. That's nineteen when he graduates, if he graduates."

"He was left back a couple of times."

"Also he's rude, obnoxious, ill-mannered and totally un-disciplined, not to mention he doesn't have any kind of a future, let alone going to college."

"He's going to be an entrepreneur like Diddy."

"An entrepreneur," Laura repeated, almost positive that he couldn't even spell the word.

"Yeah, he's an event promoter."

"An event promoter? Is that considered an occupation nowadays?"

"Yes, and he's gonna rap too."

"A rapper? Oh, please."

"You say that like it's a bad thing."

"Do you hear yourself talking?" Laura asked. "I just listed five things wrong with that boy and you haven't heard a single word I said, and now his only redeeming characteristic is that he wants to be a rapper."

"Dad likes him."

"That's because he plays football."

"He could get a scholarship."

"I've seen him play. He's not that good."

"I don't know why you always hating on him."

"You could do better."

Tamika didn't respond. She knew her mother was right. She just didn't want her to know it. And anyway, this conversation was moot 'cause they'd already broken up.

"Fine," Laura said, giving up on another never-ending circular battle. "Is that what you're wearing tonight?"

"Yes," Tamika said sternly.

"And your hair?"

"I like my hair like this, Mom."

"But it's—"

"It's what I like, Mom. No perm, no curls. It's natural and I want it like this."

Stalemate, their conversations always ended in a standoff, each firmly and unwaveringly standing on opposite sides. Laura just nodded. "Come on, sit down. Dinner's ready and your father and I have some news for you."

"News?" Tamika asked.

"Yes, news," Laura said, going back into the kitchen.

"What's the news?" Tamika asked, dreading the answer. She remembered that the last time her mother and father had news for her, it was to tell her that they were separating and that her father was moving out. That was a year ago and luckily it only lasted a few weeks.

"After dinner," Laura said, returning with a bowl of mashed potatoes and a dish of warmed-up homemade beef gravy.

"Can't you tell me now?"

"No, after dinner. Did you wash your hands?"

"Mom, I'm sixteen years old, not three."

Laura looked at her and half smiled. She was right; she wasn't three years old anymore. And in two years she'd be going off to college and then after that married with her own home and family. A sudden sadness shadowed Laura's face as she thought about all the missed opportunities. So much time had passed and she wasted most of it working in an advertising office and not with her family.

"So, what's for dinner?" Tamika asked, following her mother into the kitchen. Seeing her father standing at the counter, opening a bottle of wine, stilled her apprehension for a while. Him already being home was odd enough, but if he was opening wine that meant they were at least speaking to each other. Still, hopefully it wasn't a divorce.

"Hey, Dad," Tamika said.

"Hey, baby," he said, smiling as he always did. "So, what do you think?"

"About what?"

"The news," he said.

"After dinner," Laura said sternly, glancing at Malcolm and smiling tightly. He nodded as she walked back out with a pitcher of iced tea.

"So, how was your last day as a tenth-grader?"

Tamika shrugged. "Okay, I guess."

"You guess? That doesn't sound too definitive."

"It was a'ight."

"How's Justin?" he asked.

She shrugged again. "He's a'ight, I guess."

"Just a'ight?" he asked. "I thought you were tight."

"He trippin', that's all, so we're chillin' for a while."

"You okay?" he asked.

"Yeah," she said with a sigh of indifference. "For real, no biggie."

"All right, come on, you two. Dinner's on the table," Laura called out from the dining room.

"Come on," Malcolm said, wiggling his eyebrows the way he always did to make her laugh, "dinner's on the table."

They went in, sat down and ate dinner. Everything was perfect as usual. During the meal they talked about nothing in particular—school, movies, television—and then over dessert Tamika asked about the news. Malcolm and Laura glanced at each other. He nodded for her to go first.

"Okay, I'll start," Laura began. "You remember that position I wanted at the advertising agency? The one where I had a second interview last week?"

Tamika nodded.

"Well, I got a call. Unfortunately, I didn't get the job."

Tamika went quiet. She'd hoped that her mother had the job for both their sakes. She knew that her mother loved working, and being laid off had been hard on her, on both of them. "For real?"

"Yes, I found out today. This morning actually. The agency decided to go in another direction."

"So what exactly does that mean?"

"Actually, I'm not really sure. I guess they wanted someone younger to groom in the position."

"No, I mean how does it affect us?"

"It doesn't. We still have a really nice severance package from before and I get to spend more time with you."

"So that's it? You're not gonna look for another job?"

"Yes, of course I will, but not right away. It's summer so I thought since I'll be away, I'd take a break with the job search for a while."

"Okay," Tamika said reluctantly. "So, you are still going to Georgia in two days, right?"

"Yes," she said, then looked at Malcolm.

Tamika turned to her dad.

"My turn," he began. "The job is sending me to Tokyo."

"Tokyo?" Tamika repeated.

"Yes, Tokyo, Japan."

"I know where it is, Dad. I'm just surprised. Are we supposed to be going too?" Tamika asked hopefully.

"No," Laura said.

"So, what about our vacation when Mom gets back?"

"We can still go, we'll just postpone it a bit."

"Can we do that?" she asked.

"Sure. It'll take a bit more planning, but I'm sure we can make the change without too much trouble."

"What if you find that the job is more detailed and you have to stay longer?" Laura asked.

Malcolm looked at her. "We'll just cross that bridge when and if we get to it."

Tamika nodded. "So, when are you leaving, Dad?"

"Next week."

"Next week," she repeated, then paused. "That soon?"

He nodded with a mouthful of apple pie and ice cream.

"So, wait, if you're going to Tokyo next week and Mom's still going to Georgia in two days, then that means I get to stay here by myself for a month, right?"

"Wrong," Laura said, quickly ending the rush of excitement in her daughter's voice.

"So, what am I supposed to be doing while y'all are both away? I have the photo camp internship starting in two weeks, remember? Don't tell me Aunt Sylvia's coming to stay. She's crazy."

Laura looked up, instantly annoyed. "I don't ever want to hear you say that again, do you hear me?"

Tamika nodded silently.

"Aunt Sylvia isn't crazy. She's a bit eccentric, that's all. She has her own ways."

"She's nuts," Malcolm muttered, getting Tamika to smile. Laura glared at him, then at Tamika.

"I didn't say it," Tamika quickly affirmed. Laura looked back to Malcolm. "So, is Aunt Sylvia coming up here or what?"

"No, she's not coming. She's already half moved out of the family house."

"Cool, so then what am I supposed to do?"

"You're coming to Georgia with me."

"What? But what about my internship? It starts—" she paused, remembering the phone message "—in two weeks. I already paid for it out of my money."

"We'll reimburse you," Malcolm said.

"But no, it's like an internship and it'll look good on my college applications."

"You'll have to pass for the time being," Laura said.

Tamika's jaw dropped. She was stunned. Obviously there was some mistake. "Pass? What do you mean pass? As in not going at all?"

"I'm sorry, sweetie, but there's really no other way."

"Wait, I've been looking forward to going to this camp internship for months. How can you just say, sorry, you can't go?"

"I'm not saying that," Laura said. "If we get back in time, then fine, but I'm not making any promises."

"So that means I'm not going, right?"

"That's not what I said, Tamika. You're hearing what you want to hear."

"You said that it'll take a month to do the house. My internship starts in two weeks. I may be only sixteen but I can do the math."

"We'll be back in time to go to Martha's Vineyard," Malcolm said eagerly, trying to appease the conversation. "And it really shouldn't take too long to get everything in order down in Georgia. I'm sure you'll be back in time for your camp," he added easily without glancing at his wife.

"It's not just a camp, Dad, it's an internship. It's preparation for college."

"Okay, fine. After that you'll be back home and have the rest of the summer."

Laura looked at him. As usual, he just didn't get it.

chapter 3

Tamika

"**what** do you mean you're not going tonight? You have to go. Duh, your boyfriend, or rather ex-boyfriend, whichever, is throwing the party of the year. The last thing you want to do is not show up. It'll look like you're broken-hearted or devastated or something."

"I don't care. Believe me, I'm seriously not in the mood to be partying right now. Just go ahead without me."

"Uh-oh. What happened now?"

"Oh, nothing much, just my whole friggin' summer is trashed and all it took was a few little words from my mom."

"What few little words?" Lisa asked.

"First of all, she took a phone message while we were at the mall this afternoon that my internship messed up and instead of starting in two days I start in two weeks. Then she didn't get the job she wanted and my dad has this stupid business trip. So, bottom line is that my photo camp internship, going to the beach, hanging out with you before you leave and everything else is trashed. I swear she loves doing this to me."

"Wait, what are you talking about? What exactly happened?" Lisa asked.

"Remember I told you that my mom was going to Georgia for a month?"

"Yeah, so?"

"Well, guess who's going with her now?"

"You, for real?"

"Yeah, me, for real."

"I thought you were gonna kick it with your dad while your mom was away. Wait, did they separate again?"

"Nah, they didn't separate again—at least not that they're saying. But he's got to go to Tokyo for a month, maybe more. That means everybody's out of the house and they don't trust me to be here alone for a month. I'm sixteen years old. I swear they act like I'm still a kid." Lisa giggled. "It's not funny, Lisa."

"I know, I'm sorry. It's just that last summer when you had the house to yourself for the week you almost got them tossed in jail for abandonment and reckless child endangerment."

"It's not the same thing. I'm older and I know better. There's no way I'd agree to let Justin throw another party like that at my house again. I can't believe I let myself get talked into it before. He couldn't do it at his regular place so I agreed. I'm still hearing about it."

"But you didn't even invite them last time either. They just came and you know what happened after that."

"Whatever, but that's not the point. The point is I wouldn't do anything like that again and they should trust me not to."

"So, because of all that you're not going tonight?"

"I'm not in a partying mood."

"So that's when you need to be out with your girls."

"I don't know," Tamika said, beginning to reconsider her decision.

"Besides, Justin is promoting this. You know you have to be there. This is a big deal and if you're not there you know one of those stupid skanks will be pushing up on him. The man will be seriously cash-heavy and you know that's all it takes."

Tamika considered a moment. She knew that Lisa was right. Whenever she turned her back there were always some skanks trying to turn Justin's head, and just in case they hadn't actually broken up...

She relented. "A'ight, fine."

Six hours later the party was popping and thankfully Lisa was right—hanging out with her friends was exactly what she needed to clear her mind. If this was the last time she was going to be around for a while, then she was going to kick it for real.

And she did. She danced and laughed and joked around all night. By the time they were ready to bounce, her ears were ringing from the loud music, her feet were hurting from dancing so much in heels and she was just plain exhausted. The party was seriously crackin'. The DJ was tight and mostly all her friends from school had shown up. Halfway through everybody started talking about Justin's next party.

"I heard your boy is talking about promoting another party next month," Lisa said as they stood to the side of the dance floor still enjoying the music.

"Yeah, I heard," Tamika said.

"You know y'all will be back together by then."

"I seriously doubt it." Tamika shrugged, then glanced across the room, seeing Justin dancing with both Drea and Lexea. She shook her head at his pitiful attempt at getting attention.

"I guess you see your girls bumping up all on your boy over there," Lisa said, leaning in for her ears only.

"Yeah, I see 'em. They are so stupid with all that dumb

stuff, and for real, do they ever do anything one at a time? They're, like, inseparable, joined at the single brain cell."

Lisa laughed. "Girl, if you still want him you'd better lock him up again or take him with you. I have a feelin' it's gonna be a long few months."

"I'm not even stressing about all that. He wanted space, he got it. I'm done."

"Uh-huh, and I know why." She glanced across the room. "Sean Edwards."

Tamika followed her line of vision. "Sean?"

"Don't be acting like you don't know. Yeah, Sean. I saw the two of you all over in the corner talkin' a few minutes ago, faces all close together and all."

"It's loud in here," she shouted to emphasize her point, "and we couldn't hear each other talk so I had to get close just to hear what he was saying."

"Oh, please, y'all ain't fooling nobody with that sly innocent stuff y'all pullin' over there."

"We was just talkin', that's all."

"Uh-huh, right, just talkin'."

"He was telling me about what he was gonna do this summer."

"Uh-huh, right, talking," Lisa said again.

"Would you stop saying it like that? It wasn't even anything like that. We was just talkin', that's it."

"Well, you better make sure that Justin knows that, 'cause he was for real checkin' y'all out just talkin' over there," Lisa said.

Tamika smiled. It was obvious that that's exactly what she wanted.

"Wait, don't tell me that you were trying to use Sean to get back at Justin."

"You saw him with Drea and Lexea."

"You can't be using Sean. He's a nice guy and he likes you."

"He doesn't even know me."

"You wrong, Tamika," Lisa said. "That ain't right."

But by that time Tamika had glanced over to where Justin was. He was still dancing but instead of paying attention to what Drea and Lexea were doing grinding all up into him front and back, he was looking at her, smiling.

"Y'all just playing that game and using Sean to get back at each other. That's so childish. Sean is really nice."

"Why don't you go out with him?"

"Hello, I'm leaving in a month and a half. Besides, he likes you, not me."

"And you know all this how?"

"Let's just say we talk and he's nothing like Justin."

"Justin. Oh, please," Tamika said, sucking her teeth and half chuckling. "I'm seriously not dealing with his drama or with any of this other crap. He's the one who acted like he wanted to do his thing, so fine, let him have it. He's the only one who started steppin' out. I'm just following by example."

"But, girl, you know how he is, self-centered and selfish. You say all the time how tired you are of him and you go right back with him."

"Yeah, and that's just it. I'm not doing it anymore. And as for Sean, we was just talking. I can't help it Justin thinks it was something more."

"So, what was y'all two talking about, you and Sean?"

"Georgia."

"Who's Georgia? Oh, you mean the big girl who was in our lit class two years ago? Didn't she move to Dallas or someplace like that?"

"No, Georgia, like in the state of Georgia."

"She moved to Georgia?"

"No, crazy, we was talkin' about Georgia."

"Oh, Georgia," Lisa said, laughing. Then she crinkled her nose questioningly. "Georgia, so what about it?"

"His family is from Georgia and not too far from Fraser. He actually knew where it was and everything. He said that he goes down to visit his grandparents every summer and that he was probably gonna visit them again this year."

"Cool, maybe when he's down there and you're down there y'all can hook up or something."

Tamika glanced over to where she and Sean had been talking. He was still standing there, but now he was talking with a few of his friends. He didn't look her way and she was glad about that. He was cool and all, but since they didn't travel in the same circle of friends they didn't really hang out with each other, so she really didn't know him. They'd had a few classes together in ninth grade and she definitely knew who he was, but they just never really talked much until tonight.

"You know what? It's starting to slow down up in here. You ready to go?" Lisa asked, taking one final glance around the crowded room. The DJ was still spinning, but it was late and it was obvious that the place was starting to thin out. It was the perfect time to leave.

"Yeah, I'm ready. Let's go."

They started to walk through the crowd toward the exit door. Just as she and Lisa got near she felt someone grab her hand. She turned, expecting to see Justin. It wasn't. Sean was standing there smiling at her. "Hey, shorty," he said. "You leaving now and not even gonna say goodbye?"

Tamika smiled and nodded. "Yeah, we gotta go."

Sean glanced at Lisa and nodded. She returned the gesture,

then casually looked away. "So I guess I'll check you out in Fraser, right?" Sean said.

Tamika smiled wider. "Yeah, okay, I'll see you in Fraser."

"I'm not joking. For real, I'll be down."

"A'ight, I believe you," she said skeptically. "See you later."

He let go of her hand and just stood there as she and Lisa continued to the exit.

"Girl, I don't care what you said about just talking. Whatever Fraser is must be tight, 'cause that guy is pressed about you."

"He was just talking. There's no way I'm really gonna see him down there. Besides, hopefully I'm only supposed to be there for a little while. If I'm lucky I'll be back in two weeks."

"I hope so. It's gonna be a long-ass summer with you gone."

"For real," Tamika said.

Lisa smiled. Their friendship was special. They'd come a long way since grade school. Archenemies at first, they instantly hated each other and then all of a sudden they were best friends. Neither one of them remembered just when or how everything changed but they were glad it did.

Tamika sighed heavily. "I still can't believe it, just like that," she said as she and Lisa stepped outside. "Can you believe it? Dad gets to go to Tokyo for a month, maybe two, and I have to go with my mother to clean out a house in Fraser, Georgia."

"Maybe it won't be so bad," Lisa said as they walked the short distance to the parking lot next door to the club.

Tamika looked at her best friend. Her response was implied and understood. "But it's not just that. Did I tell you that we'll be driving down? Can you believe it? We're not even flying. I looked it up. It's over a thousand miles. That means twenty hours in a car with my mother and nonstop nagging." She started laughing. Lisa joined in while shaking her head, commiserating with her friend. They got to the car, got in and waited as usual..

It never failed, there was always somebody who had to park all crazy and block at least six other cars. Tamika and Lisa talked generally about the party, then about the last day of school and the summer. By the time they could finally drive off they were laughing their heads off about Justin, Drea and Lexea.

At the first traffic light Lisa stopped and turned to Tamika. "So, wait, hold up. How big is it?" Lisa asked.

"How big is what?"

"The house you gotta clean out," Lisa said, glancing over quickly at Tamika's confused expression.

"Oh, um, I don't know. I have no idea. The last time I was there I was, like, nine years old. I don't even remember the place."

"So all you have to do is clean it out, right?"

"Yeah."

"So, whose house is it anyway?"

"I think it was originally the house my great-grandmother grew up in, like, a hundred years ago. Then my grandmother lived there with my granddad's sister after he died. Then when my grandmother died a few years ago my great-aunt lived there, but now she's moving out to live in one of those senior citizen apartments near her daughter. Now my mom wants to sell it herself, so we have to go down there and clean it out. It's nothing but a bunch of old junk there anyway, but my mom still wants to check it out."

"Old junk? Girl, you seen those antiques shows on PBS. Y'all probably have a book sitting up in there that's worth half a million dollars or something or a chair that Prince Somebody sat on and got crowned."

"What? Yeah, right, uh-huh. Girl, you crazy," Tamika said, not taking Lisa seriously.

"No, really. Seriously, you need to really check it out when you get there. You don't know what you'll find up in there. That stuff happens all the time. You remember that guy who found a copy of the Magna Carta or the Declaration of Independence behind this old picture he bought at a flea market? He got like a billion dollars or something. See, it could happen."

"That's just an urban legend."

"Nuh-uh, for real it happened."

"Well, not to me. That stuff's probably just a bunch of old junk that nobody wants," she said.

"Still you should check it out. So, what are you gonna have, a huge yard sale or something?"

"I don't know, that's my mom's job. She doesn't really need me there. She just doesn't want me here alone."

They drove in silence for a few blocks.

"I just can't believe this," Tamika repeated. "She said that I wasn't mature enough to stay home alone."

"She actually said that?"

"Not actually, but it was the same thing. I don't get it. She wants me to act mature but she won't give me the opportunity to show it. Ever since she got laid off she's been impossible. I can't wait to get out of there."

"You can always write your college application essay about this trip."

"Yeah, I can just see myself doing that. How I spent my summer vacation trying not to strangle my mother, by Tamika Fraser."

They laughed as Lisa pulled up in front of Tamika's house. "A'ight, I'll talk to you later."

"Okay, I'll call you tomorrow," she said, then got out and

went into the house. The kitchen light was on, so of course she headed upstairs to her bedroom. She'd missed curfew by half an hour.

"Tamika, is that you?" her mother asked.

"Uh-huh, I'm home. Sorry I'm late. We got blocked in."

"Are you hungry?"

"No, I'm just gonna go to bed."

"Come here for a minute. I want to talk to you."

Tamika groaned inwardly, knowing that's what her mother wanted all along. She went into the kitchen and saw her mother sitting at the kitchen table with a bottle of water in front of her. "How was your evening? Did you have a good time?"

"It was okay," she said, looking away disinterestedly.

Her mom nodded. "Tamika, is it too much to ask for a little consideration?"

"I'm not doing anything," she said, crossing her arms over her chest. "And I said I was sorry about being late but it took forever to find the person that parked wrong and was blocking everybody in. We all had to sit there and wait for him to move his stupid car."

"Okay, fine. How about a little conversation?"

"Okay."

"Why don't you have a seat," Laura said.

Tamika sat down at the center island counter.

"Look, sweetie, I know this whole thing is disappointing for you. Believe it or not I'm disappointed too. But sometimes we don't have a choice. We need to do things that we'd rather not. Circumstances give us no alternative."

"Yeah, I know."

"We'll drive down, clean the house out, put it on the market and then come right back home. Hopefully your dad will be back by then so we'll go right to the beach, okay?"

"Yeah, okay," she said.

"I realize that you were looking forward to this camp."

"Photo camp internship," she corrected. "Yes, I was, and just like that it's gone."

"Circumstances require that we sometimes—"

"Yeah, I know, Mom, circumstances, right?" she interrupted.

"If you have something to say, Tamika, say it."

"This internship was important to me, Mom. It was my chance to shine and to maybe get my work published. But instead I have to go someplace to clean out an old house. It's not fair. But I'm sure you don't understand that. How could you? You're an adult."

"Of course I understand that, Tamika. I was a teenager too at one time."

"Could have fooled me. I wish for once you'd remember what it's like to be sixteen."

"Be careful what you wish for. You just might get it."

"Fine, I'd welcome it, a chance to be an adult, make my own decisions and follow my own rules."

"It's not as easy as it seems. Adults don't have it any easier than teens. There were things that are important to me too but—"

"See, there you go. There's always a but, an exception. This was important to me and you don't even care."

"Of course I care. It's just that some priorities—"

"See, there you go. You don't care."

"As I was saying, some priorities take precedence over what we want, Tamika. It's called growing up. As you get older and more mature you'll realize that. At times you just have to step up and do what needs to be done even if it means doing what you don't want to do."

"So why can't I stay here by myself, then?"

"I think you already know the answer to that."

"Yes, fine, I messed up. It was a stupid decision that got out of hand, no big deal."

"No big deal? It was irresponsible and reckless."

"But still, that was a year ago. I was a kid and most of it wasn't even my fault. And besides, the neighbors and the police overreacted anyway."

"Tamika, the kitchen was on fire."

"It was just the countertop."

"And the floor and the table, two chairs and the refrigerator. I still have no idea how that could happen. I didn't even know it was possible."

"That could happen to anyone."

"But it didn't, it happened to you. And it wasn't just the countertop, it was half the kitchen. I would know because we had to have it completely redone."

"Fine, I can stay with Lisa until she leaves. You'll be back by then."

"Tamika, you were supposed to be staying with Lisa last year too, remember? I suppose that's when the idea of having an unchaperoned party occurred to you."

"It wasn't my fault. It wasn't supposed to happen like that."

"You invited over a hundred teenagers here. What exactly did you think was going to happen? I'm sorry, the answer is no."

"Fine," she said dryly.

"Attitude isn't gonna make this trip any easier on either one of us, so you can drop it now."

"What attitude?"

"That sulky attitude of yours."

"I'm not sulkin', I'm just tired. It was a long day."

"Okay, fine, my mistake. But all I'm saying is that maybe we can use this time together to have fun, just the two of us. We haven't done that in a long time. I know I've been busy with work and all, but now that I have the time we can use it to really enjoy ourselves."

"Okay," Tamika said.

"We'll be leaving day after tomorrow so if you have things you need me to pick up let me know. I need to go shopping first thing tomorrow. I have a list started on the refrigerator, so add whatever you need."

Tamika turned to the list, then nodded. "Okay."

"All right, that's it, good night."

"Night," Tamika said, then left. As soon as she went up to her bedroom and closed the door, her muted cell buzzed.

Lisa: \(^_^)
Tamika: (^_^)/
Lisa: I went 2 Sean's myspace
Tamika: ?
Lisa: He posted about 2nite
Tamika: ?
Lisa: About U

Tamika didn't type anything right away. She just sat there trying to figure out what Sean wrote about her. Expecting the worst she turned on her laptop.

Tamika: me?
Lisa: check it out

Lisa ended the message. Tamika typed in her MySpace password, then went to Sean's page. She was surprised; it was nicer than most, different. But then he was always a pseudo–computer geek. It was actually kinda tight. She scanned through, checking out what he said about her.

so I went to this party tonight. it was poppin' and all and the music was a'ight. but the best part was that I got to re-connect with this girl I knew from way back. she was different but the same. she supposed to be with this guy but I don't know about tonight. maybe they're done. maybe not—either way it's a'ight wit me. yeah. But she could do better. I should've gotten her digits. next time.
—Sean

After reading it Tamika smiled. She knew it was about her. So since her MySpace had her photo she opened another account with a picture of a star, then responded.

Yeah, you should have gotten her digits. next time.

chapter 4

Laura

The Frasers lived in a quiet suburban neighborhood located just outside of Boston. Unfortunately the peace and quiet of Ambrosia Lane was exactly what she didn't need right now.

Now two days later, on the morning they left for Fraser, the day had started off with drama. Packed and ready to go, Laura was in the car waiting for Tamika. She'd expected a full-scale rebellion and that's exactly what she was getting. Subtle and clever, Tamika still got her message across. She was not happy.

She'd been waiting for fifteen minutes. She was just about to go back in the house when her cell rang. Scrambling through her purse, she answered. "Hello."

"Hey, I just called to see if you were on the road yet," Malcolm said.

"I'm outside the house waiting for your daughter. She's been dragging all morning. You'd think she'd appreciate the beauty of the drive. But no, not her," she said as she adjusted the cell phone to the other ear.

"Just give her time."

"Easy for you to say," she said.

"She's out of school so you won't be fighting over grades and schoolwork. This should be a breeze. She really wants to spend time with you."

"Yeah, right. What world have you been living in for the past three years?"

"The two of you will hang out together like before."

Laura just shook her head. Before was a long time ago. Then she'd take Tamika to the zoo, art museums and concerts and shopping in New York City. Now she wouldn't even think about trying that.

"Well, at least you'll have a break," she said.

"Come on, Laura, let's not start this again. This is necessary, right? You were gonna go down anyway. Taking Tamika is the logical thing to do."

"Yeah, I know. It's just that she's so sulky. I swear she's driving me crazy," Laura said. "I try to be nice but all I get is attitude."

"Give her time," Malcolm answered on automatic, having had this same conversation before.

"All I'm saying is that when I was a teen I was overjoyed to get away from home for a while, but no, not your daughter. Everything I do she does the exact opposite."

"Laura, you know how Tamika is, she's a teenager. You remember being a teenager. Our parents didn't know anything either. As teens we were invincible and immortal. We knew it all. Now multiply that feeling by a million and you have today's teenager. Compared to us at that age they're far more mature. She's doing what every teenager did since the beginning of time—being a teen."

"Yeah, I know. She's spoiled, selfish and self-centered. I

swear she only thinks about herself. She really needs to grow up. She'll be going to college in two years and then what? She won't even tie her shoestrings without me telling her to."

"Maybe you need to give her more credit. She'll step up when she needs to and you let her."

"You keep saying that," Laura remarked. "See, that's why she's like this. You baby her."

"I baby her?" Malcolm exclaimed. "Me?"

"Yes, you. You give her everything she wants. No wonder she doesn't want to go to Georgia with me. She knew that she could get away with anything she wanted staying here with you."

"You know you tripping now, Laura. If anything you spoil her. You need to give her some slack."

"How can I? See, look, I told her to be ready to leave an hour ago. We should have been on the road thirty minutes ago. I hope she's not still in bed. Letting her hang out last night was a huge mistake. I told her to be home early and she came rolling in after midnight."

"Laura, chill. Time isn't cut in stone. You gotta relax. So what? You hit the road a few minutes later than you planned? So what? She hung out last night? She was only hanging out at the mall and movies with her friends."

"The mall closes at nine," she said.

"The movie theater closes late," he said. "And I'm sure she's on her way out right now."

"She's probably in there talking with Justin."

"No, I think they broke up."

"What? When?"

"A few days ago, I think. She didn't tell you?"

"No."

"See, that's why the two of you need to take this trip

together. You need to reconnect again. She's going to be going off to college in a couple of years and the two of you need this time. Think of it as the last hurrah before launching her into the real world."

"College," Laura droned. "Oh, don't remind me."

"I know, seems like she was just crawling around here in diapers."

"What are we going to do when she's gone?"

"Exactly what we're doing now," Malcolm said, then quickly changed the topic. "How's the car rental?"

"Nice, very nice," Laura said, smiling.

"What'd you get?"

"Something more suitable for the drive down," she said, looking over the car approvingly.

"I still don't see why you didn't want to drive your minivan down there. It would have been roomier, more practical and so much easier than renting a car."

"Maybe, but certainly not as much fun," Laura said, smiling brighter as she continued to look over the newly polished fire-engine-red convertible Mustang.

"All right, listen. I gotta go," he said as he nodded to his assistant standing at his open office doorway. "Have a good trip. Call me tonight."

"Okay, bye." Laura closed her phone, feeling the useless feeling again. "Figures." She bemoaned another meaningless conversation with a husband who was more interested in straight lines on a blueprint than straightening out their marriage.

She loved Malcolm but somewhere along the line they just didn't connect anymore and she'd stopped living and started merely existing. He was always nose-deep into job specs and cost projections. That's all he did with occasional pit stops into their lives. At work all day, then working at home all night, he stayed immersed in a constant state of distraction. She just couldn't compete anymore. She wasn't sure if she even wanted to.

Their separation a year ago, although a wake-up call to problems, hadn't really changed anything. The problems they had then still festered below the surface of silence now. She wasn't happy and apparently he still didn't get it.

So this was her life. At thirty-nine she was forever stuck in a never-ending cycle of family drama. She shuddered. Marriage wasn't supposed to be this hard. Her parents had been happily married for over forty years. They worked together every day and barely had a cross word.

Her father died three years ago, then her mother a year later. She loved her parents and had a great relationship with her mother. They were best friends. Why couldn't she have that kind of relationship with her daughter? Was that asking too much?

She needed a change and with or without Tamika with her this trip, she intended to do something to shake her life up.

Moments later, still distracted, Laura hadn't noticed Tamika walk up to the car. The tension immediately rose. "You rented a car?" Tamika asked, surprised.

"Yes, like it?"

"A bright red convertible."

"That's right," Laura said happily.

"What's wrong with your minivan?"

Laura shrugged. "It's too me."

"What's that supposed to mean?" Tamika asked as she tossed her small carry-on bag in the backseat, then opened the passenger side door and got in.

Laura smiled without answering. "So, hey, you ready for our adventure?"

"Not really," Tamika said truthfully, sliding in beside her mother and checking out the dashboard gadgets.

"Oh, come on, you might just have some fun and even learn something in the process," Laura said, deciding to try and charge a bit of excitement into the road trip.

"I doubt it," Tamika mumbled.

Laura started the engine. It hummed, ready. "Ah, summer, sunshine and the open road. What could be better than that?" she said, then sighed as she pulled out of the driveway.

"Oh, I don't know. How about staying at home chilling, maybe?"

Choosing to ignore her cynicism, Laura continued. "I went online and picked out some really nice places to stop and eat and a cool bed-and-breakfast."

"A bed-and-breakfast for what?"

"We're going to spend the night, unless of course you prefer to just stop on the side of the road and sleep in the car," Laura said.

"No, but spend the night? Why can't we just drive straight there and get it over with?"

"Because I have no intention of driving twenty-something hours straight," she said.

"I can drive too," Tamika said, for the first time excited about the possibility of being there.

"I don't think so."

"Why not? I have my driver's license, Mom. Remember, you cooked a celebration dinner the day I got it."

"I know you have your license, Tamika, but this is highway driving. It's not just running around the corner to grab a soda from the store or going to the mall with Lisa."

"I've driven on a highway before, Mom. My driver's ed instructor took us out. It was part of the curriculum. And then Dad let me drive on the parkway and highway."

"That was driving around Boston. This is different."

"Mom..."

"Tamika."

"Fine," Tamika said, knowing she wasn't getting anywhere. "Okay, I get it. You don't trust me."

"I didn't say that."

Tamika didn't answer; instead she reached over and turned on the radio, then searched for something more to her liking. She found a station and turned the volume up loud.

Laura moaned and glanced over at Tamika.

Tamika looked away, then out the side window.

"Is she supposed to be singing?" Laura asked.

"Who?"

"Whoever that is on the radio," Laura responded.

"You don't know who that is?" Tamika asked.

"No. Is it the young girl that got the career-achievement award on the award show a month ago?"

"Which award show?"

"Oh, right. There were at least half a dozen music award shows on television last month. What were they, video awards, audio awards, rap awards, non-rap awards, I'm-out-of-jail awards, gold-teeth awards?"

"Very funny," Tamika said sarcastically. "And FYI, gold teeth are out."

Laura chuckled. "No, seriously, this girl won a career award after two or three albums. I think she was, like, nineteen or twenty years old. I mean, really, a lifetime-achievement award. Come on now."

"See, there you go again, dissin' my music. And by the

way, they don't make albums anymore. That's old, old school."

"Tamika, even you have to admit that's ridiculous. Now, what was her name?"

"I have no idea who you're talking about."

Laura looked over to her daughter and smiled. Obviously that conversation wasn't working. "Okay, fine, you can narrow it down by who's not arrested or in jail this week."

"Oh, please, like the people you listened to didn't have drama in their lives. Don't even let me have to bring up that I know you had a crush on Michael Jackson when you were growing up." Laura didn't rebut. "Uh-huh, that's what I thought. You can't answer that, can you? And you know that man's drama."

"Fine, granted, there's drama in just about every generation of singers, okay?" Tamika nodded. "Good. Okay, so who is she?" Laura asked as the song started to go off.

"Dang, Mom, she's, like, the biggest R & B singer out today. You seriously don't know?"

Laura shook her head. "Never heard her before."

"You really need to get out more."

"Well, if she could actually sing and not holler and scream, then maybe I would have heard of her."

"She's not hollering."

"Well, she certainly isn't singing. Chaka Khan, Anita Baker, Regina Bell, Phyllis Hyman, Gladys Knight, Natalie Cole, they sang. I don't know what this child calls herself doing but it certainly isn't singing."

"See, you always ridin' my music."

"I wasn't putting your music down. I thought we were having an insightful, intelligent conversation."

"No, you were telling me that my music was crap."

"How in the world did you get that from what I said?"

"'Cause that's what you said."

"That's not what I said."

"Never mind, whatever," Tamika said abruptly, then turned off the radio, pulled out her earbuds and adjusted her music.

"You used to love this, us hanging out, talking about things, even debating issues, remember?"

"No," she said, and then turned on her music.

Laura could tell she was lying but it didn't matter. Tamika was already into her music by the time they reached the main highway out of town. It was obviously going to be one of those days, but Laura refused to get annoyed. This was her trip and she planned to make the best of it, with or without her daughter.

After that, their disconnection grew more evident as the miles rolled by and the car remained silent. They stopped for a break in a small town outside of New York, then stopped again for lunch just outside of Philadelphia. When they got to the Washington, D.C., area, Laura exited the highway and drove through the city.

She pointed out several major landmark sights, hoping Tamika would share some enthusiasm. She didn't. She just nodded and went back to what she was doing.

Following directions she'd mapped out to Arlington, they drove down a brick pathway leading through massive open gates surrounding the immaculate landscaping of Arlington Cemetery. In the distance Laura spotted their destination. She pulled up then drove into a parking area.

"Why are we stopping here?" Tamika asked.

"Come on," Laura said when she turned to see Tamika still sitting in the car.

Tamika looked around. "I think I'll stay here."

Laura glanced at her and was just about to say something

but then decided not to. This was her trip and she intended to do what she wanted, with or without her daughter. "Fine, stay, I'll be back."

She walked down a narrow path, then into a large white building. A few minutes later she came out with a piece of paper and got back into the car.

"Why are we going in here?"

"To see someone," Laura said.

"Why are we here?" Tamika said, hoping it wasn't what she knew.

"Come on, let's go," Laura answered.

Tamika didn't answer but she did get out and follow her mother as she entered a huge white and tan rotunda-shaped building. They passed through the other side, which overlooked rolling hills and D.C. monuments in the far-off distance.

There were shuttle tours available, but most people just mingled and walked around quietly on their own.

"Mom, can I wait here?" Tamika asked. Laura nodded and kept walking.

All white marble and identical with either simple block lettering or just a noted number, they looked like miniature soldiers standing at attention. With paper in hand Laura walked down several narrow paths until she found what she was looking for. She stopped, then walked over. She knelt, spending several minutes in reserved silence just looking down. It wasn't until she stood again that she realized that Tamika was right behind her.

"Somebody you know?"

"Yes," she said, then paused. "Okay, next stop. Let's go." Tamika rolled her eyes.

Alexandria, Virginia, was next.

Laura drove through the narrow streets smiling at the new scenery. "I always wanted to come here."

"Why?" Tamika asked.

"I don't know. I guess it's the history or pageantry of the nation's capital."

"Boston's prettier. I think we have a better—eww..." Tamika said, turning with her nose crinkled. "Did you see that?"

"See what? No, I'm driving, what was it?" Laura asked, glancing around quickly.

"Eww," Tamika repeated.

"What, what?"

"Those two guys back there, did you see 'em?"

"No, why? What about them? What did they do?"

"They were checking you out," Tamika said.

"Checking me out, huh?" Laura said, chuckling. "Somehow I doubt that. They must have been looking at you."

"Mom, I know when someone's looking at me, and those two guys were for real looking at you."

"Old toothless bums, right?"

"No, they were businessmen in nice suits and they were like Dad's age, maybe younger even."

Laura, still driving, glanced up in the rearview mirror. Of course, she had no idea who these two mystery men were, what they looked like and where they went, but she half smiled anyway, feeling pretty good. Moments later she pulled into a parking lot, grabbed her notebook and stuffed it into her purse. "Come on, let's check it out."

"Do we have to? Can't we just..." Tamika said, then looked at her mother. "Never mind." She got out of the car.

They walked down a brick sidewalk crowded with pedestrians and tourists, then stopped and poked around in a couple of small boutiques. "Is this all they have here, old stuff and antiques?"

"What's wrong with old stuff and antiques?"

"Kinda lame, don't you think?"

"No, not really. But if you prefer, there are other shops around. Plus there's the Torpedo Factory by the river. Do you want to check that out?"

"Ah, never mind, I'll pass. I'm not in the mood to see a bunch of torpedoes."

"There aren't any real torpedoes. It's just the name of the building because of what they built there years ago. It's a crafts mall now. They have jewelry, designer clothes, paintings, things like that. I think you can even watch the craftsmen at work."

"Nah."

"They have a couple of photography studios," Laura said, knowing that would certainly pique her daughter's interest.

"Okay, maybe we can stop by for a few minutes."

They stayed over an hour. Tamika got to talk to some professional photographers and even someone who freelanced for the *National Geographic* magazine. When they finally left, Tamika was definitely feeling better.

"Okay, let's go this way," Laura said, holding her map of the local area. They walked beyond the stores and shops to a more residential neighborhood, then through to a remote area.

Tamika focused her camera and snapped a few shots as they walked. Laura stopped at an old church as Tamika took a few more photos. Happy with the still compositions she'd been seeing, she continued shooting.

Using the lens as her eyes, she followed her mother. "So, when exactly are we gonna get back to civilization?"

"Come on."

"Are you sure you know where we're going?" Tamika asked. Laura kept walking, heading down the narrow path to the gated area a few yards away. She stopped.

"Uh-uh." Tamika looked up and paused. "I know you're not talking about us going in there."

"Of course we are."

"Mom, do you see a recurring theme happening here?"

"Tamika, it's just stones and earth."

"Mom, it's a graveyard—again. Our second graveyard of the day, in less than, like, three hours. Dead people live here, you know."

"Since when are you afraid of dead people? They can't hurt you."

"I know that. That doesn't mean I'm going out of my way to hang out with them all day either."

"Oh, come on, girl. I want you to see something."

Tamika studied the surrounding area. The ancient stone crumpled up through the earth on a jagged, toothless mound. The artistry of the setting prompted her to refocus the lens. Through digital pixels she found her timeless narrative.

"Come on," Laura said.

"Again?"

"Yes, again," Laura insisted. She tried the rusted gate latch. It opened easily. "Good, it's not locked."

"Of course not. Who would lock a cemetery gate? It's not like anyone in there is getting up and walking out, and who in their right mind would want to go inside? Oh, wait, that would be us."

"Very funny," Laura said as she opened the creaky, creepy iron gate and walked inside. It was still early but the sky was overcast and an eerie gloom surrounded them as they stood there alone with the dead. Laura started walking. Tamika didn't move. Laura looked back, seeing her still standing at the entrance.

"Come on," she said quietly.

"Where?"

"Here, inside," Laura said, standing in front of an old beat-up gravestone. She looked around, quickly reading the headstones.

Tamika focused her lens and took a few shots. "Are we supposed to be in here?"

"It's a public cemetery."

"So why are you whispering?"

"Respect," Laura said.

"I don't think they mind," Tamika said as she glanced around the open space. "What exactly are you looking for?"

"Shh, keep your voice down," Laura said.

"Why? It's not like we're gonna wake anyone up," she said, then chuckled.

Laura looked back at her daughter. "Just have a little more respect, please, okay?"

Tamika sucked her teeth and looked away, rolling her eyes. "Whatever." She glanced around the small overgrown cemetery and crinkled her nose. This road trip was getting crazier and stranger by the minute. She turned to watch her mother continue to walk in and out between the headstones.

"What are you doing?" Tamika asked as she came closer.

"Just wait," Laura said.

"What, uh, who are you looking for?"

Laura didn't answer. She'd apparently found who she was looking for. She walked over, bent down to clear the debris away from the front of the stone. She reached into her purse and pulled out a flashlight.

"Yep, here it is. Come here, read this."

Tamika moved closer, leaned down over her crouching mother, read the names, then nearly fell back, getting away from the stone. She shrieked.

"Shh," Laura said.

"What is that?" Tamika nearly screamed.

"Be quiet. We don't want the whole world over here."

"You said this was a public place."

"It is, but still..." Laura said as she unfolded a piece of tissue paper and began rubbing the stone with a lead pencil.

"What are you doing?" Tamika asked. Laura didn't answer. Tamika repeated the question, obviously knowing exactly what her mother was doing. "Ewww."

"It's history, Tamika. Our history."

Moments later she finished her rubbing and they left, closing the gate securely behind them. Back in the car, Tamika shuddered. Laura looked over at her daughter before starting the car. Maybe now was a good time to take a break.

chapter 5

Tamika

TAMIKA couldn't relax. The creepy feeling had stayed with her even after they arrived at the bed-and-breakfast just a few miles outside of Alexandria. Her mother had already made reservations, so they checked in and went directly to their waiting room. Small and cute, right next to the water, with two bedrooms that were both pink and frilly, it was definitely not her style. But it was okay and at least it wasn't near a cemetery, at least none that she saw.

She checked out the typical amenities, television, computer jack, mini refrigerator and balcony overlooking what was probably the Potomac River. It was all standard stuff. The one thing that did stand out was the connecting bathroom with a serious Jacuzzi tub and steam shower.

After a day on the road with her mother, and visits to two cemeteries, she could seriously use time to herself to chill out. After checking out the tiny combined seating area, Tamika took the smaller bedroom. She went in, dropped her overnight bag, purse and laptop backpack on the bed and walked over to the window. Looking out, she watched a bustle of people as they busied themselves with their lives.

"At least you have a life," she muttered. This was even worse than she had thought it was going to be. "A cemetery, a cemetery, you have to be kidding me," she added, still muttering to herself. She stood there awhile, then heard her mother quietly knock on the open door and come in.

"Please tell me that was the last one," Tamika said.

"The last what?" her mother asked.

"Cemetery," she said, turning around to face her mother who'd walked over to the window to stand beside her.

"It was the last one," Laura said, looking down at the view, then at her daughter. "Are you okay?"

"Yeah, it was just weird, that's all," Tamika said.

"Different yes, but weird, I don't know. Maybe you just have to be a bit more open-minded or mature to appreciate it."

"I am mature. Just 'cause I don't like hanging out at cemeteries all day doesn't make me immature."

"It wasn't all day and I meant emotionally mature. You still have a lot to learn, Tamika. You're just sixteen."

"You know, you say that all the time when you want to justify doing what you want to do."

"Oh, really?" Laura said.

"Yes, really," she said. "It's true, you do. You make it seem that your life is more important than mine so your plans take precedence."

"Like the photo camp, I presume?" her mother asked.

"Exactly like the photo camp internship. You knew I really wanted to go, but still what you want is what we had to do. You act like I have no idea about my life but I do. I know what college I want to go to, what I want to major in and where I want to work when I get out. I may not be perfect like you but I do have some things in place."

"Perfect, me?" Laura asked.

"Yes, you, perfect. Everything you touch is perfect so don't even try and front like it's not."

"Tamika, I have no idea where you've been but as of six months ago I got laid off. No employer is knocking down the door to hire me at thirty-nine years old. My husband is more interested in his career than in his marriage, my daughter thinks I live my life on cloud nine and I have to drive a thousand miles to go back to the place I never wanted to see again. That's not what I call a perfect life," she said, then shook her head and continued.

"I know it seems that you have all the answers right now, but believe me, Tamika, you still have a lot to learn. Sixteen is still very young and I'm not saying that you're a child. In the past year you've matured tremendously. You're a beautiful young lady and I'm so proud of you."

Tamika moaned. Even her mother's arguments were perfect. Fine, sure, as usual she was right. She had matured since last year, but nearly burning the house down had a tendency to do that to you. Either way that wasn't the point. As usual their conversation was moot as far as she was concerned. Her mother was never going to see anything her way; she was just too old and set in her ways. "So, what were you like when you were my age? Were you emotionally mature?"

"I had to be."

Tamika had heard the "life was so hard when I was your age" parental war stories so many times she could recite them verbatim. She wasn't in the mood to hear them again. "Mom, all I'm saying is for you to at least try to remember what it was like being my age once in a while."

Her mom nodded and smiled. "Sixteen, huh? That was a long time ago, but I'll tell you what." She paused. Tamika prepared for another letdown or at the very least another lecture on growing up and being more mature. "I'll try," she said, smiling.

Tamika was shocked. Her mother actually conceded. "So I suppose there was some deep important lesson or reason for what we did today, right?" she questioned.

"Yes, there was."

"I think I need to take a shower and get something to eat before I hear it, okay?" She shuddered, thinking about the last creepy old cemetery.

"Okay, you go first," Laura said, then walked back into her bedroom while still talking. "I'm gonna run downstairs and see if I can find a nice place to eat. I think we deserve to celebrate." The door opened, then closed.

Tamika sighed, walked over to the bed and sat down. It was firm with two fluffy, overstuffed pillows. She lay back looking at the ceiling and thinking about her day so far. It definitely wasn't what she had expected. But then again, it could have been worse.

A week ago, she was in school taking the last of her final exams, and here she was tonight, hundreds of miles away, lying on a bed wondering what in the world she was doing. She closed her eyes and took a deep breath. Feeling the pull of sleep, she sat up quickly when she heard her cell phone ring. Not recognizing the phone number, she answered anyway.

"Hello?" There was no reply. "Hello?"

"Tamika, hi."

"Who's this?" she asked.

"It's Sean. I hope you don't mind that I'm calling you. I

got your phone number from Lisa. I had to promise her three college essays to get it."

Tamika smiled. Usually she would just hang up when someone called her out of the blue like this. Being popular in school unfortunately attracted every wannabe jerk wanting to hang on and she wasn't having that. But since it was Sean and he was cool she decided to chill. "Hey, hi. Yeah, I was just wondering how you got my cell number."

"I know, not cool, but since you didn't offer it to me the other night I figured I had to get creative, so don't be mad at Lisa. She held out."

"Yeah, but for how long?"

"You really want to know?" he asked.

"Yeah," she said, "tell me."

He laughed a little, then went silent as he cleared his throat nervously. "Um, okay. I've tried to get her to give me your phone number since ninth grade."

"Ninth grade? So why didn't you just ask me?"

"I know, my bad. I guess I was just shy back then."

"And now I guess you're not shy anymore."

"Well, after we talked the other night, you seemed..."

"I seemed what?" she asked.

"Look, we gonna talk about all that now or you want to talk about something else?"

Tamika could hear the nervousness in his voice, so she let the conversation drop. "Okay, so you called me. What do you want to talk about?"

"I was just wondering how you liked Fraser so far."

Tamika looked around her bedroom. "We're not there yet. I'm at a bed-and-breakfast in Virginia."

"Virginia?"

"Yeah, we stopped in to chill for the night."

"That sounds cool. Are you enjoying the drive down?"

"Not really. So far we've stopped at two cemeteries. I can't wait until tomorrow. My mom probably has us lined up to stop at a haunted house or something."

He laughed. "Okay, so what you doing hanging out at cemeteries? I didn't think you were into the goth thing."

"I'm not. My mom's straight trippin', that's all."

"So you'll be there tomorrow, right?"

"Yeah, I think so. Why?" she asked.

"'Cause I want to see you when I get there."

"So, for real, you're actually coming down here?"

"Yeah, told ya that's where my family's from."

"A'ight, call me when you get down there."

"I probably won't be there until July."

"Oh well, hopefully I'll be back in Boston by then."

"I thought you were staying longer."

"I hope not," she said.

"So what's so important here in Boston? Justin?"

"No," she said quickly.

"So, y'all two together or what?"

She sighed loudly. "I don't know. I guess I'll pick the *or what*."

"Good," he said.

"Why you say it like that? You got beef with Justin?"

"Nah, I just think you could do better."

"Oh, really? Got anyone better in mind?"

"I got a few ideas. I'll let you know," he said playfully.

"Okay, you do that," she said sweetly.

"A'ight. So I'll check you later."

"Okay."

"Bye."

Tamika hung up smiling. Sean was nice and she liked

talking to him. First it was out of necessity 'cause at the party Justin was all up in somebody else's face and she wasn't about to be standing there looking all stupid. So when Sean started talking she just hung with it. But now she kinda liked talking to him. He had a nice voice and he was interesting. He made her laugh.

She picked up her camera and began going through the photos she'd taken earlier. Some of them strangely enough were pretty nice. She'd gotten some real good ones at the cemetery in Washington. There was even a nice one with her mother walking through the one in Alexandria. The sun was perfect and the color washed through rich and vibrant. She wondered what she'd be doing if she'd gone to the photo camp internship. Definitely not taking pictures of cemeteries.

A few minutes later she got up, grabbed her small overnight case, pulled out some clothes, popped out her contacts and went into the bathroom. Twenty minutes later she was feeling great. She dressed and sat outside on the small balcony texting Lisa.

Tamika: Hey!
Lisa: wassup?
Tamika: noth-N U
Lisa: jst chill-N
Lisa: how's the drive?
Tamika: don't ask
Lisa: 4 real that bad?
Tamika: worse
Lisa: LOL R U there?
Tamika: no
Lisa: where R U?

Tamika: VA B&B
Lisa: nice?
Tamika: okay—Sean called
Lisa: I was gonna tell U bout that
Tamika: Uh-huh
Lisa: I know—sorry—y'all talk?
Tamika: Yeah, he's cool
Lisa: C
Tamika: he's coming down
Lisa: nice
Tamika: I'll let U know
Lisa: Stop—he's nice
Tamika: I know
Lisa: Give him a chance
Tamika: We'll C

"Tamika, you ready for dinner?" her mother asked, stepping out onto the balcony after taking her shower and changing her clothes too.

"Yeah, I'll be right there," she called out behind her.

Tamika: GTG
Lisa: K CUL8R
Lisa: have fun
Tamika: Grrr!
Lisa: LOL

They left the bed-and-breakfast and walked a block and a half to the restaurant. It was empty so they got seated quickly and ordered. Dinner was surprisingly good. They ate and chatted a bit, then just walked around before heading back to the bed-and-breakfast.

"So, did you enjoy yourself today?" Laura asked.

"It wasn't as bad as I thought it was gonna be."

"So you enjoyed yourself, then, huh?"

"I ain't say all that. It was interesting, I admit that. But I seriously would not say that I enjoyed myself."

"Fine, agreed."

Laura smiled. It was the first time since the beginning of the drive that the two of them had agreed on anything.

"Okay, so why the cemetery tour?" Tamika asked.

"I did the same thing with my mother when I was just about your age."

"And you liked it?" Tamika asked. Laura didn't reply right away. "Uh-huh, see that? Same as me, right?" she said, pointing and laughing at her mother.

Laura laughed too. "Okay, okay, let's just say it wasn't my cup of tea at the time but I appreciated it. It was my history, my family. And that's always important," she said. She looked over to Tamika, trying to gauge her receptiveness. "It was something we shared and it kind of brought us together, made us closer. So I hoped I could share it with you like she shared it with me." Tamika just nodded. Laura considered that the best she was going to get.

"You said that it was our family. How so? I mean, I get the names and all but what else?"

Laura told Tamika about her great-grandmother's grandmother who was a slave and the mistress of her master. She had several kids with him when his white wife died. When he died he freed her and their children together, then gave her the land in Fraser, his family land.

They walked and talked a bit more as Laura answered questions and listened to Tamika. After a while they turned to go back. "Okay, now how do we get out of here?" Laura asked.

"You don't know?"

"I have no idea. Wait, there's the river that's behind the bed-and-breakfast. Let's go that way."

They walked along the river path beside the Potomac and within a few minutes they were back in front of the bed-and-breakfast. "So, how much longer before Fraser?" Tamika asked.

"About ten hours or so."

When they got back to their rooms they each said good-night and headed for bed. Tamika crawled in and lay waiting for sleep to come. It didn't, not for a long while.

chapter 6

Laura

After a pleasant enough evening and a good night's sleep, Laura was back to finding her peace.

They'd eaten a filling meal at the bed-and-breakfast, then got on the road sooner than expected. She filled up the gas tank and they were back on the highway in the now usual position—Laura driving, enjoying the ride, and Tamika plugged into her music and texting her friends from time to time.

A few miles out Tamika pulled out her earbuds. "So, where are we stopping today? Ghost house, chamber of horrors, or are we gonna cut to the chase and witness a good old-fashioned hanging or beheading?"

"Very funny," Laura said sarcastically.

Tamika chuckled aloud. "I thought so."

"No, today I thought we'd do some shopping."

"Shoppin' for real?" Tamika said, brightening up.

"For real," Laura said.

"Cool, it's about time."

"I thought you'd like that idea."

Tamika nodded and smiled. She could get into that. She plugged her earbuds back in, relaxed back and waited to do some serious shopping.

Laura smiled and silently chuckled over that joy that mothers got when they told the truth but not the whole truth. What was said and what was assumed were two different things. A few hours into the drive Laura pulled off.

"Are we here?" Tamika asked after nodding off the past hour or so. She looked around. "Wait. What is this place?"

"Shopping," Laura said simply.

"This isn't shopping. When you said we were going to shop I thought you meant for-real shopping at a mall or something, not this stuff. What is this place?"

"It's an antique and open flea market."

"You're kidding me, right?"

"Nope," Laura said happily.

"Mom," Tamika said, obviously disappointed, "never mind."

There were hundreds, maybe thousands, of people already milling around open stalls and dozens of tables that ringed the perimeter of the massive outdoor space.

Laura drove a bit, then luckily found a parking space close to the opening. She pulled in quickly and got out. She turned, seeing Tamika still sitting there with her arms folded across her chest. Without a word Laura turned and started walking away. She was determined not to let Tamika ruin her day.

She stopped at the first booth she came to and quickly looked over the myriad gadgets on display. She walked to the next booth, then the next and eventually fell into a rhythm as she quickly glanced over the offered wares and either kept on walking or paused to take a closer look.

By the time she'd rounded several corners she was completely immersed in the overwhelming sense of joy. She was having fun. She'd forgotten how much she used to enjoy rummaging through antique shops and early-morning flea markets. She passed a small booth, quickly scanned it, then continued but stopped a few feet away and retraced her footsteps. She stood at the table examining a box of old Victrola vinyl.

"What are they, albums?"

She turned, recognizing the voice. Tamika stood beside her, looking at the table, peeking into the box. She reached over and pulled out a black disc and examined it closer. "Isn't it too thick to play on y'all's old record player?"

"It's not an album for a record player. These are for a Victrola."

"What's a Victrola?"

"It's something like the first record player but it was called a talking machine back then."

"A talking machine?"

Laura nodded as she picked up another record and examined it. "Your grandmother had, or rather, has, a Victor Victrola Cabinet phonograph. I think these might play on it. It's a beautiful old machine made out of mahogany with I think twenty or thirty cylinders or something. It used to work great."

"It still works? How old is it?"

"About a hundred years old, give or take a few."

Laura smiled as Tamika's jaw dropped. "We got something that old at the house?"

"Sweetie, we got a lot of things that old at the house. Some much, much older."

"Are they worth anything?"

"Maybe. I guess we'll have to check and possibly have a few things appraised."

"So, what are we gonna do with them?"

"I don't know yet, we'll see."

Laura bought several of the records, then took the seller's card in case she decided to purchase more. Tamika lagged back for a few booths as Laura continued walking.

A few stalls later Laura was talking to a woman about a lamp when Tamika came over hurriedly. "Mom, come here. You gotta see this."

And just like that the day had changed. They walked side by side laughing and talking about the strange, the weird and the unusual finds surrounding them. They stopped and ate hot dogs at a vendor, then slowly strolled back to the car. With the roof up they loaded their surprising number of purchases into the trunk and headed back to the highway.

Somewhere along the way Tamika had fallen asleep again, 'cause when she woke up the top was down and Laura was singing and nearly dancing out of her seat. Tamika half smiled; she had no idea who this woman was.

Laura glanced over. "Hey, sleepyhead, welcome back."

"What are you doing?" she asked, looking at her mother.

"What do you mean?" Laura asked between bouts of off-key singing.

"I mean, what are you doing?" she repeated.

"I'm singing. Duh," Laura said.

"But this isn't your music."

"Why not?"

"'Cause it's a Chris Brown remix."

"A Chris Brown what? Remix?"

"Yeah, a remix. So how do you know the words?"

"'Cause this song, Miss Remix, was out when I was in high school and I used to love it. I used to dance to it all the time. I haven't heard it in forever, like twenty years or so. I forgot all about it."

"Get out! No way, this ain't no twenty years old."

"Oh yeah, way," she said, trying to sound equally cool. "My dear, this was my jam," she said, then hollered along with the song to make her point.

"Your what?" Tamika asked. "What's a jam?"

"My jam. You know, my song. This was a hit back then," she said, then reached over and turned the radio up, blasting Chris Brown from the car speakers.

Tamika burst out laughing. Her mother was a trip sometimes when she was trying to act all cool.

"Come on, sing with me, baby," Laura said, grabbing Tamika's hand and holding it up in the air. Tamika shrugged. They sang and sang and sang some more. Cars and trucks passed as they continued singing. Some blew their horns, smiled and laughed as others just drove by thinking that they were probably nuts. But it didn't matter because for the first time in a long while mother and daughter were having a ball.

"That was nice. What else does he sing?" Laura asked.

Tamika unplugged the earbuds from her MP3 and connected it to the car jack on the dash. She pushed a few buttons on the small device and music blasted out through the car speakers.

Laura started boppin' her head. "Heeey," she said, and as her shoulders got into the mix, in a few seconds they were right back at it again.

"Is this Chris Brown again? What's it called?" Laura asked.

"It's the 'Run It' remix with Chris Brown, Bow Wow, and Jermaine Dupri. It's old, from a few years back, from his first CD," Tamika said.

Laura listened a few seconds as her head continued

bopping. "I like it, I like it," she yelled as she reached over and turned up the speakers, blasting the music even louder. "It's cool."

"No, Mom, it's hot," Tamika corrected.

"Oh, okay. I like it. It's hot, then. We should get it."

"Get what?"

"Get this."

"Mom, I already have it," Tamika said as she laughed at her mother.

"Heeeyyy."

Tamika cracked up laughing as she watched her mother listening to her music and liking it. Apparently hell had just frozen over.

"Heeeyyy."

Tamika still laughed as her head started boppin', her shoulders started rocking and she raised her arms, letting the wind blow her hands in a constant wave.

A car came driving up alongside them, and the passenger, hearing their music, leaned out and started smiling and waving and bopping her head to the music from their car.

"Heeeyyy." Laura glanced over and smiled as everybody in the car started rocking to the remix looping all over again. Tamika cracked up as both cars rocked past the next two exits.

So with the top down and still rockin', boppin' and singing at the top of their lungs, Tamika and Laura arrived in Fraser, Georgia, just before dusk, still pumped up and enjoying their music.

It had rained earlier and the streets were still damp. A mugginess hung heavily in the air, and a thin layer of mist surrounded them, dusting the streets and threatening to roll in as fog.

"So, this is it?" Tamika asked, sounding more disappointed than excited.

"You've been here before."

"Yeah, when I was nine. I don't remember all this."

"Nine? What about— Oh, that's right. You and Dad didn't come to the funeral, did you?"

"No, remember we had the flu and a bad cold? I thought I was gonna die," she quipped, then paused and looked at her mother. "Sorry."

Laura glanced at her as she drove. "For what?"

"Saying that."

"Saying what?"

"That I thought I was gonna die, since your mom and dad actually did die."

"Sweetie, it's okay, don't worry about it." Tamika nodded. Laura smiled. Her daughter had actually apologized for the possibility of upsetting her feelings. She considered that a good sign, that maybe this wasn't such a bad idea after all. "You hungry?" she asked.

"Yeah, a little," Tamika said, realizing that they hadn't stopped since their early lunch at the flea market.

"Well, I'm starved. Let's get something to eat before we head in. What do you feel like?"

"I don't know, whatever."

"You know what, there used to be this incredible barbecue place about a mile or so down the road. Feel like some ribs?"

"Sure."

Laura kept driving as she started checking the place out. "Wow, look at this place. It's like going through a time warp. Everything looks exactly the same," she said as she pulled off the road and parked on a gravel lot in front of the barbecue restaurant. She turned the engine off and they got out.

"This is it?" Tamika asked, thinking that the place looked like a run-down dive.

"Yep, this is it," Laura said. "The best barbecue in the world, except for mine, of course."

"It looks like it's closed."

"It always looks that way. Come on, let's go inside."

Laura led, walking the gravel path to the front door. She opened it and stepped inside. Tamika followed. As soon as they walked in, the aroma of mouthwatering smoked ribs and sauce made their stomachs growl. "Umm, this place smells incredible," Laura said.

Tamika hated to admit it but her mother was right. It smelled like heaven and the place was packed thick. It looked as if half the Georgia population was inside the small restaurant.

A young woman with a clipboard walked up to them smiling. "Two? Y'all want a booth or a table?" she asked, her Southern accent thick. "It's gonna be at least a forty-five-minute wait either way."

"We're getting takeout," Laura said.

"Y'all call it in already?"

"No."

"'Kay, here's the menus," she said, handing them two laminated folders. "Y'all can place your order at the counter over there."

Laura and Tamika looked over the menu, decided, then placed their order. They stood waiting, looking at the dessert case, trying to decide what else to buy.

"Laura Hopkins?"

Hearing her maiden name, Laura turned around. "Yes."

"Don't you dare tell me that you don't remember me. It's me, Grace. Grace Hunter from Fraser High. Although I guess I should have called you Laura Fraser since you went back to your original, original name."

"Grace," she repeated. Then, like a light turning on, her face brightened. "Oh my God, Gracie," Laura squealed. "I can't believe it's you. How've you been?"

Tamika moaned inwardly. Her mother was a talker and given half the chance she'd probably be standing there all night talking to everyone in the place. Tamika looked at the woman hugging her mother and half smiled. She definitely didn't look as though she'd be a friend of her mother's. Round, fleshy and comfortably full figured, she had to be her mom's age but she was dressed as if she were still in the 1980s.

"Girl, I been all over the place but I'm just fine now. I'm single, you know. Oh yeah, I finally divorced that no-good fool I had dragging me down. His mama had a fit when I sent his tired ass packing back to her. So, girl, the only thing I got on my mind these days is fun. That means a cold drink and a hot man."

Laura cracked up and Tamika just stood there. She couldn't believe that this apparently wild woman was once her mother's friend. They were as different as night and day.

"Oh my God, girl, you still as crazy as ever. So, how long has it been?"

"It's been forever, girl. So, what are you doing here? Where are you staying?"

"We're staying at my parents' house. We came down to clean and close it up to sell."

Grace nodded. "I heard about your mom. I'm sorry. She was good people. We all adored her. I was out of town when she passed and missed you when you came down. I sent a card but I don't know if you got it."

"I got it and thank you."

"So you're selling the house yourself now?" she asked.

"Yes, hopefully we can put it on the market before we leave. My aunt Sylvia is moving out now. But to tell you the truth, I have no idea what the place even looks like anymore."

"As your neighbor down the road, around the corner and a few miles away, I can tell you that the place still looks good. But it always did."

"That's good to hear. Oh, wait a minute. I want you to meet my daughter, Tamika. Tamika, this is Grace Hunter, an old schoolmate and my bestest friend in the universe since Clark Elementary School."

Grace burst out laughing. "Lordy, child, I haven't heard that line in forever, my bestest friend in the universe. Yep, that was us," she declared. "Hello, Tamika, nice to meet you. Girl, you look just like your mother did when she was your age."

Tamika half smiled. As far as she was concerned she looked nothing like her mother.

"How old are you?"

"Sixteen."

"Sixteen," Grace repeated. "Oh, to be sixteen again."

"I know, wouldn't it be great?" Laura said.

"What grade are you in?"

"I'm going into eleventh grade in September."

"Eleventh grade. Lordy, they grow up so fast, don't they?" she said, leaning into Laura and chuckling. Laura nodded. Tamika just looked at both of them as if they were nuts. "My youngest son is a few years older than you and I still can't believe he's already in college. But between you and me I'm glad he's gone. Lordy, that boy was driving me crazy. Had all those hot-behind wannabe hoochie mamas calling my house day and night. Near about drove me crazy."

Laura cracked up laughing. Grace joined in until she looked over, seeing her companion waving to her from across the room. "Lordy, I better get back over there. That man's 'bout ready to break his arm off if I don't get my butt back over there."

"You are exactly the same," Laura said.

"Yeah, right, and about a hundred pounds overweight but I'll take the compliment. But, girl, look at you. You look like you walked right out of high school yesterday."

"Liar," Laura said, giggling.

"Mom, I think our order's ready," Tamika said as the counter person called their receipt number and placed a large plastic bag on the counter.

"Okay," Laura said, then hugged her friend and promised that they'd get together.

"Y'all go ahead, I'll see you later. Call me, I'm at the same phone number. We can maybe hang out while you're here," Grace said.

"Okay, sounds good. I'll do that," Laura said.

Grace went back to her table and Laura paid for their takeout. After stuffing the bag with extra sauce, plates and plastic utensils, Tamika grabbed the bag to leave. Laura turned for a brief second, seeing Grace waving at her from across the room. She waved back, then followed her daughter to the exit. "I can't believe that I forgot all about her. After I left college I guess I forgot all about a lot of things."

"So, that was a friend from high school," Tamika said as they got back into the car with their food.

"From elementary, middle and high school, yes. There were four of us—Grace, Francine, Judith and me."

"She doesn't quite fit your style."

"No, I suppose not. We each had our different strengths. We kind of grew apart over the years."

"That's one thing Lisa and I are never going to do, lose touch with each other."

Laura nodded and smiled. That was the same thing the four of them had promised each other almost thirty years ago.

chapter 7

Tamika

THey'd eaten dinner and then cleaned up.

No dishwasher—Tamika still couldn't believe that.

While her mother talked on the phone to her dad then to her aunt Sylvia, Tamika walked outside to get some fresh air. The house, at the end of what was called Diamond Point Road, was huge with a lot of land and woods behind it. Closed up for nearly four days, it was stiflingly hot and she thought that if she stayed inside any longer she was sure she'd spontaneously combust. Unfortunately it was just as hot and uncomfortable outside.

The night sky shone bright as stars and planets dotted the velvet mass above her. Crickets and frogs and cicada and whatever else sang in the hot musty air. It had drizzled again, leaving the air thick with moisture and heat. The fog that had threatened earlier rolled in slowly, dusting the black asphalt with a gentle haze.

Tamika, sitting on the front wooden rail, picked up the extra paper plate she'd been carrying around ever since they'd arrived with the food and fanned herself. The disturbed air felt good but not good enough. How could anyone live without central air?

"Hey, what are you doing out here?" Laura asked through the screen door.

"Nothing. I'm just sitting looking at the sky, at how clear it is here. You can see almost every star."

Laura opened the screen door, walked outside, sat down beside her daughter and looked up. Crickets and other critters sounded in the darkness.

She sighed. "Man, I forgot about this part. I used to sit out here late at night sometimes and just stare up at the sky. My dad even bought me a telescope and I kept a journal and everything."

"Really, a journal?"

"Oh yeah. I was big into writing in my diaries at one point. As a matter of fact, I wanted to be a writer."

"But you stopped writing, right? So what happened?" Tamika asked.

"I guess I grew out of it. I made more money copywriting for advertising. Although, you know what? I think that telescope is still upstairs in the attic someplace. Do you want to bring it down?"

"Nah, maybe later," Tamika said, knowing that there was no way she was gonna lug a telescope around as hot as it was. "So, what do people do around here for fun? Speak all countrified while eating vittles like chitterlings and pigs' feet and shooting each other?"

"What? Where did you get that?"

"I don't know, this is the country, isn't it?"

"This is Fraser. I don't know where you're talking about. We have cars and CD players and hip-hop and cable TV and DVDs and everything else the rest of the country has."

"But no dishwasher and air conditioners," Tamika said.

"There are air conditioners all through the house, just no central-air system."

"What's the difference? Hot is hot."

Laura opened her mouth to rebut, but she couldn't argue the fact. It was definitely hot. "Well, maybe you have a point there, so just maybe you'll learn to appreciate all the little amenities you do have once you get back home."

"Speaking of which, whose car is that out front?"

"Never mind," Laura said quickly.

"Fine, so where's Aunt Sylvia? I thought she was gonna be here when we got in."

"She's probably visiting a friend. I'm sure she'll be back soon. Do you know why they call this Diamond Point Road?" Laura asked. Tamika shrugged. "It's because when the family started selling off the land generations ago, it was sold in diamond shapes. This house is the point of the first diamond."

"I don't get it. So, if General Joseph Fraser was so in love and left everything to his black wife and we're her descendants, then shouldn't this family have more than this house?"

"Do you really think that the rest of his family and the good people of Fraser would allow a former slave to own land, let alone be a widow to a white man?"

"So they stole the land back."

"It reverted to his family and they gave her just enough land to work. Their biggest compromise was that she and her children remained free. I guess that's all she really wanted in the end."

"That's wrong."

"That's life."

Tamika looked around and sighed. "Two weeks, right?"

"That was your father's idea. I doubt very seriously that we're gonna be able to get this place ready to sell in just two weeks." Laura's cell phone rang just as she finished. She checked the caller ID. "It's your dad again."

Tamika stood up. "I'll be inside."

Laura opened her cell and answered.

Tamika went back into the kitchen and grabbed a bottle of water from the refrigerator. It had been a bother at the time, but now she was glad that her mother insisted they stop by the local grocery store and pick up a few things after they left the barbecue restaurant.

She opened her bottle and walked around checking things out again. It had been a long time since she was there; everything looked new or rather old. After checking out the first floor she decided to get a better look at the second floor. She climbed the stairs and started opening the doors. Each room, dark and musty, was more depressing than the last. She finally got back to her bedroom, went inside and sat on the bed, opening her cell at the same time.

She left a message on Lisa's cell, then debated about calling Sean but decided against it. She wasn't sure if she was ready for that yet. She finished her water, then went back downstairs and looked around. "Mom?" she called out as she stepped out onto the porch, but didn't get an answer.

She went to the kitchen, then back upstairs. "Mom?"

"Up here," Laura called out.

Tamika climbed the narrow stairs to another floor and walked down the short hall. The door was open at the end. "Mom?"

"Yeah, in here."

Tamika walked in and looked around, then spotted her

mother sitting on the floor with several open boxes around her. "Dad okay?"

"Yeah, he says hi and that he misses you. Why don't you call him later? I told him that I would call back tomorrow, but I'm sure he'd like to hear from you."

Tamika nodded while looking around. "Dang, didn't y'all ever throw anything out?"

"Doesn't look like it, does it?" Laura said.

Tamika peeked into a box, seeing a stack of magazines and newspapers. "Y'all saved old newspapers?"

"Special newspapers, headlines," Laura said. "When World War Two ended, when the space shuttle *Challenger* exploded, when President Nixon resigned, when Martin Luther King and the Kennedys were assassinated, things like that. My mother collected newspaper headlines all her life."

"Really? Huh," Tamika said, slightly interested. "What about the magazines?"

"Um, I think she had the first issues. Like *Time, Newsweek, Life,* things like that."

"So, are they worth anything?"

"Maybe, possibly to collectors, I guess."

"Cool, we should sell 'em."

"Let's first see exactly what we have, okay?"

Tamika walked over to stand beside her. "What's all this?"

Laura sighed contentedly. "Memories, dreams, hopes, disappointments, trash."

Tamika looked around. "Is any of this stuff worth anything like antiques or something?"

"Maybe. I guess we could get some things appraised. I think there are a few antique stores in town."

"So, what exactly are you supposed to be doing?" Tamika asked, seeing shelves lining the perimeter of the attic walls and everything neatly arranged and in labeled boxes—clothes, schoolwork, photos, etc.

"Actually, I started off looking for my telescope and my journals but then I found all this."

Tamika looked down at the huge mess her mother had made in the middle of the floor. There were open boxes and piles of clothes and books all around her, including a pile of jeans and T-shirts on the floor beside her.

Tamika reached down and picked up a pair of jeans. She held them out to see better. "Oh, check, whose are these?"

Looking up and seeing the jeans Tamika held up in front of her, Laura said, "Mine."

"For real, these are yours? since when?"

"Oh, since about 1978 or so, I guess."

"But these are seriously in style right now. They're vintage. You can only get them in specialty boutiques and online and even then they cost a fortune."

"My mother always said there's nothing new under the sun. If you wait around long enough, everything comes back in style again."

"Calvin Klein, Gloria Vanderbilt, Jordache jeans... I can't believe it. I've been looking for a pair of these in stores for the last few months now. Nobody has them yet." She held them up to her hips and chuckled. "I bet they fit perfectly."

"There's another box of clothes over there. You might want to check it out," Laura said. Tamika nodded. It took some digging around in several other boxes, but for the next twenty minutes she tried on at least ten pairs of jeans. Checking herself out in the mirror, she admired the way the clothes fit her so well. Although they were all dusty and musty, it was like finding diamonds in a coal mine. Totally unexpected but seriously well worth it.

"They look good on you," Laura said.

"Can I wear them?"

"Why don't we wash them first? They've been stored in these plastic containers for over twenty years."

"Okay." She gathered the jeans and put them by the door to go downstairs to the clothes washer in the basement.

Tamika walked back over and picked up a T-shirt from another pile. She held it out, then chuckled. "Where'd you get this?"

Laura looked up and smiled. "Grace and I went to their concert a hundred years ago. That's before they were really popular, then broke up and became music moguls and a preacher with his own reality show. I bought a T-shirt with my allowance and I think Grace got a cap. We climbed up onstage, danced, then Grace got Russell's phone number as we left."

"Get out, y'all did that?"

"We did that," Laura affirmed.

"Wow, I seriously can't see you doing that."

"We did, but that was a long time ago."

"Wow."

"Yeah, wow."

"What about this T-shirt?"

"Yep, went to that concert too."

"So, how come you don't do that now?" Tamika asked, poking her head into a box sitting on the floor beside her mother.

"What, climb onstage at concerts?"

"No, I mean acting cool like that."

Laura shook her head, amazed by her daughter. "You are so bold and defiant. I envy that. Your life is laid out in front of you with every possibility available. All you have to do is reach out and grab it."

"No way, it's not that easy," Tamika said.

"Of course it is."

"No, you have the perfect life. You do what you want, when you want, nobody to tell you what you have to do," she said as she poked her head into another box.

"It's not perfect, Tamika, trust me."

"What's this?"

"Gimme that," Laura said, reaching out for it.

Tamika held it away. "No way, this is your yearbook, isn't it? I want to see it." She opened the book and started laughing almost immediately as she began checking out the stately statuesque photos lined across the pages.

Laura, now ignoring her, busied herself digging into another box.

"Oh, trip, look at y'all. This is you, right?" Tamika asked, turning the book around so that her mother could see it.

"Yep, that was me all right."

"Check out your hair. Look familiar?"

"It was a bad hair day."

"Nah, don't even try it. It's the same style I have now and you know it," she said, then continued turning the pages and seeing all the autographs and sentimental salutations written throughout the book. "Ooh, who was this?" she asked, turning the book around again.

Laura glanced up, then instantly smiled bright. "That was Keith Tyler, all-star football player, quarterback, team captain, crowned prom king and of course most popular guy in school," she said, then continued digging in the box. She pulled out several thin books and began reading through the pages.

"He's cute, so…"

Laura looked up again. "So what?" she questioned.

"So what about him?"

"What do you mean, what about him?"

"He wrote this in your yearbook, so what about him? I thought you said a million times that you didn't have a boyfriend when you were in high school."

"I didn't."

"Well, I beg to differ," she said, then cleared her throat to begin reading the quickly written scripty writing beneath his photograph. "To my heart, I will always remember you no matter where I go or what I do. You will always be in my thoughts." She looked up from the book, awaiting an explanation. "Well?"

"Well, he wrote the same exact thing in every female's yearbook."

"For real?" Tamika asked.

"Yep, for real. It might have been easier if he'd just gotten a rubber stamp and had us all stand in line."

Tamika chuckled at her mother's quip.

Laura didn't. She remembered at the time feeling too thrilled that he'd written something so personal in her yearbook. But it wasn't long before every girl in the twelfth grade started bragging about the exact same thing.

"Ooh, look at this," Tamika said, showing the book again. Laura scooted closer. They spent the next twenty minutes going through the book in detail.

The calendar receded and the years fell back as the two sat enjoying the photos of the past, making memories for the future.

Later Tamika sat in her room still looking at her mother's yearbook. She still couldn't believe she had done all those things. She pulled out her laptop and was just about to blog on her MySpace when she got an IM.

Sean: hey, U N Fraser yet?

Tamika: yeah, we got here 2night.

Sean: what do U think?

Tamika: 2 dark, I'll check it out L8R.

Sean: It was nice talkin 2 U B4

Tamika: yeah, ditto

Sean: I saw U'R myspace response—star

Tamika: how'd U know it was me?

Sean: good guess

Tamika: uh-huh

Sean: I noticed U didn't fill out my survey.

Tamika: 2 busy.

Sean: do it now.

Tamika: still 2 busy.

Sean: doing what?

Tamika: talkin' 2 you.

Sean: LOL I'll wait.

Tamika: No, L8R

Sean: promise

Tamika: promise

Tamika: when R U comin down?

Sean: 2 wks mayb, why, miss me

Tamika: just 1-dering

Sean: miss me?

Tamika: just 1-dering

Sean: LOL

Tamika: gtg, L8R

Tamika stopped IMing and went to Sean's MySpace with the survey he mentioned. She read through the questions. It was about the same as most online surveys.

The perfect date: last day of school
Your favorite color to wear: white
Hottest body part on a guy: eyes
Biggest regret: no regrets
Favorite room in the house: my bedroom
Favorite food to eat alone: popcorn
Favorite beverage: orange soda
Peas: NO!
Ice Cream: chocolate
Favorite season: summer
Can't live without: cell phone

As soon as she finished and sent it she got another IM. It was Sean again. They chatted online for almost half an hour this time. Tamika realized that Sean was nothing like the guy she thought she knew. He was funny and understanding and she really enjoyed being with him before and chatting with him now. They were still talking when her cell buzzed. She checked the caller ID. It was Lisa.

Tamika: I gotta go.
Sean: U deserting me again.
Tamika: sorry—Lisa's on my cell.
Sean: U owe me
Tamika: owe U what?

Her cell buzzed again and she picked up quickly and immediately asked Lisa to hold on a minute, then went back to Sean.

Sean: I'll think of something
Tamika: like what?
Sean: I'll let U know

Tamika: K C U
Sean: L8R

"Hey, girl," Tamika said as soon as she logged off with Sean and picked up her cell.

"Are you busy?"

"Nah, I was just IMing Sean."

"Sean," Lisa said, drawing his name out. "Ooh, Tamika and Sean sitting in a tree, K-I-S-S-I-N-G. I forget the rest."

"Good, 'cause I don't want to hear it. It's way too early for that crap. Besides, we're just friends, that's all."

"Friends, huh?"

"Yeah, friends, so stop acting crazy."

"I'm not acting crazy. Last I heard you were using him to get Justin back."

"I was not. We was just talking at the party. I wasn't using him exactly."

"A'ight, whatever. So, how's it going?"

"We just got here tonight."

"I thought you said that it only took twenty hours."

"My mom decided to do the scenic tour."

Lisa started laughing, knowing that there had to be more coming. When Tamika and her mother got together, there was always drama.

"Oh, and there's more. We stopped at Arlington Cemetery to see her grandfather's tombstone. Then we went to Alexandria to check out another cemetery. This time it was from, like, the eighteen hundreds or something like that. It was the white guy that owned the family."

"What?"

"No lie, my maternal ancestor's last name was Fraser because the man who owned one of our ancestors was named Fraser. He was some big-time general in the Civil War. So anyway, we go to this cemetery and there are our names etched into this old beat-up tombstone."

"What do you mean your names? Like your last name?"

"Yeah, plus the general's wife was named Tamika Fraser and his eldest daughter was named Laura Fraser."

"Get out."

"Talk about freaky."

"Eww, creepy-spooky. Your names were actually there except switched? The mother was the daughter and the daughter was the mother?"

"Yeah, it's just by coincidence that my mom married my dad with the last name Fraser too. That's why her family is from Fraser, Georgia. The whole town was named after this general's family even though he's buried in Virginia."

"So why's he buried in Virginia and not in Georgia?"

"'Cause he was a Union general and not a Confederate one."

"Huh? I thought everyone in the South was a Confederate."

"Me too, but evidently not. This General Joseph T. Fraser went against his family in Georgia because he fell in love with one of his father's slaves. After the war he went back and to please his family he got married, but his white wife died in childbirth. He kept the affair going with the slave and had, like, ten kids with her.

"When most of his family died from, like, the bubonic plague or the flu or something he built a house, then moved his slave family in. The slave woman he loved was named Tamika and their first child was named Laura. When he got sick he freed all his children and left them the land, but his family and white neighbors wouldn't bury him and his black wife in Georgia, so they were buried in Virginia."

"Damn, that's some serious history."

"I know."

"So, you're, like, doing U.S. history while you're there."

"Oh, but wait. Then yesterday my mom told me that we were going shopping, so I'm, like, I'm cool with that, but the next thing I know we're pulling into a huge parking lot with all these stalls and barns. She took me to a flea market."

Lisa was laughing her head off.

"I hate when she does that read-between-the-lines crap, and would you please stop laughing. It's not funny."

"Yeah, it is, 'cause she gets you all the time."

"I wish my mom was more like yours."

"Why?" Lisa asked.

"'Cause your mom is cool," Tamika said.

"That's 'cause she lives over three thousand miles away and it's the beauty of divorce. Believe me, when I go live with her in California now it'll be the exact same thing like with you and your mom."

"I wish for once she would just hear what she sounds like and what it feels like to be me," Tamika said.

"Yeah right, switch places, like that's ever gonna happen," Lisa said.

"Yeah," Tamika commiserated, "like that's gonna happen."

"So, tell me about Sean," Lisa said, changing the subject.

"There's nothing to tell."

"So, what'd he say exactly?"

"We was just talking."

"Yeah, you said that before."

"Well, you gave him my cell number. What did you expect us to be doing?" Lisa didn't say anything. "Uh-huh, that's right. You can't say anything, can you?"

"Girl, Sean was bugging from day one. He's been asking

me for your number for a long time. And since you wasn't seeing Justin…"

"Yeah, a'ight, whatever. So, check this out. At the cemetery I got these serious shots. I'm talking perfect. They're, like, right out of *National Geographic*."

"So you should send them in."

"No way."

"Yeah, do it. You see that all the time, captions from freelance photographers."

"Yeah, but those are professional freelance photographers, not sixteen-year-old high school juniors."

"You should still try it."

"I don't know, but anyway, tomorrow I think we're supposed to be getting started. Oh, wait, I forgot to tell you," Tamika began excitedly, "my mom was singing a Chris Brown song, knowing all the words and then we were up in the attic and she has all these old concert T-shirts."

"What kind of concerts?"

"All kinds of concerts."

"Your mom?"

"Yeah, seriously. And you know that else? The exact same hairstyle that I have right now, she had the same one when she was my age."

"Really?"

"I couldn't believe it," Tamika said. They started laughing.

"So, what did y'all do after you got there?"

"We ran into one of my mom's old school friends and she is seriously outrageous. It looks like she was time-warped right out of the seventies, clothes, hair and all."

"What?"

"For real, no lie, this place is a trip."

"So, what y'all have to do now?"

"I don't know. Pack everything up, I guess, or trash it all."

"How much you gotta do?"

"The whole house, everything."

"Damn."

"Yeah, tell me about it. My dad said that it would take something like two weeks, so we'll see."

"How you gonna pack everything in two weeks? I've been packing for a month and I'm still not done and I only have my bedroom to do."

"Well, that's what they said, so I guess that's it. I figure we'll be out of here around the first week in July."

"Cool, you can still start your internship."

"Yep, that's exactly what I planned."

chapter 8

Laura

Laura knew she was dreaming, mainly because she was actually happy and having way too much fun. She was in a park or meadow beneath the stars at either sunrise or sunset. Music was playing, something soft and melodious. She was dancing with Keith Tyler, her high school crush. Slow-dancing and it was nice. They weren't saying anything, just dancing and smiling. He was holding her and rubbing her back and she was just standing there letting him.

Well, maybe not letting him. She was actually telling him to do it. And each nonverbal instruction made her feel better and better. She heard herself moan as she instructed him to kiss her neck. Obedient, he did as he was told. It was nice. She gave further instructions and he did exactly as told. It was great, the complete and total control over something. Her life felt unbelievable, which is why she knew she was dreaming.

She woke a few minutes later feeling troubled. Although

the dream was pleasant enough she felt weird being married and dreaming about another man. Sigmund Freud wouldn't have any problem analyzing that dream.

Maybe it was all the drama with Malcolm or being back home or maybe it was going through her yearbook the night before, but either way it was strange thinking and now dreaming about Keith. She hadn't seen or heard anything about him in years, not since he left professional football.

After a quick washup she got dressed in her jogging sweats and was just about to head downstairs when her cell rang. "Hello."

"Hey," Malcolm said, "how'd you sleep?"

"Fine, you?" Laura yawned.

"Okay. I'm at the office now. I decided to get in early. So, how does the place look? I forgot to ask last night when we spoke," he said.

"Exactly the same."

"What about the house?" he asked.

"It needs a lot of work. I'd forgotten how run-down it was. But aside from that, everything is exactly the same."

"Was the electric and water still on?"

"Yes, Aunt Sylvia left them on just as I asked."

"Still want to sell it yourself?"

"Yeah, I think so. I don't know what else to do with it. I don't want to deal with a Realtor, but to tell you the truth I'd love to keep it in the family. After all, it is the family home from over a hundred years ago and maybe—"

"Okay, um, listen. I found out this morning that they want us to leave earlier. I have a flight out to Tokyo in two days," Malcolm said, interrupting her conversation.

"What happened?"

"I don't know yet. I know that their server crashed so

there's no computer service there at all. But I'll have my cell with me and if you need me call me."

"We'll be fine," she said coolly.

"Are you okay about this?"

She smiled. "You gotta do what you gotta do, right?"

"You didn't call me back last night."

"It was late and I figured you'd be working anyway."

"I was but I still missed hearing from you. I was worried. I tried to call, left a couple of messages."

"I forgot to charge my cell. It shut itself off," she lied easily, knowing that she purposely didn't answer or return his call because she just didn't want to deal with him.

"Laura, are you okay?"

"Yes, fine."

She could hear Malcolm's hesitant pause from the other side. She knew that he wanted to say more, but he didn't want to get into anything so he just let the conversation go.

"So, how's the cleaning going?"

"We haven't really started yet. It's only been a few hours."

"I know but I figured you'd be halfway done by now."

"Malcolm, cleaning out a house, a full house like this, takes a lot longer than a few hours."

"I'm joking, I'm joking," he said, chuckling. "I know you have a major job ahead of you. I'm just glad you have Tamika down there to give you a hand. I know you wanted to do it yourself before, but to tell you the truth I was a little worried about that."

"What do you mean?"

"I was afraid you wouldn't be back. Then when I found out about Tokyo…"

"I'll be back, Malcolm," Laura said.

"Look, I know we've slipped into that same rut again. I see it. And I know it's mainly my fault. But I—"

"Malcolm, we can't do this over the phone."

"I know, I know, I just want you not to make any decisions while you're away. I mean—"

"I know what you mean and I won't."

"Promise?" he said.

"Yeah, promise."

"Good. So, how's your daughter?"

"My daughter?" she asked.

"Your daughter. I imagine she's still sulking, so that makes her your daughter now. I'm joking."

"Not funny. But actually she's fine. We were up in the attic last night going through some things. We were listening to some music and she was trying on some of my old clothes. Apparently Jordache jeans are back in style again."

He started laughing, and she joined in unexpectedly. They started talking about the seventies, the eighties and the good old days. It was one of the best conversations they had had in a long time.

The rest of the morning was quiet. Tamika had slept late and she let her. There was no real hurry to get anything done. She had all summer. She went for her run, but it was already too hot to be out. Still it felt good to get back to a normal routine. She ran before work every morning, not necessarily to keep fit although that was working, but also to clear her mind and still her thoughts.

She got back and Tamika was still locked up in her room. Again she let her be. After a quick shower she dressed in shorts and a cotton top and went back out.

Knowing that the kitchen was bare and the refrigerator was empty prompted her to start moving. She'd go to the grocery store, to the bakery and then to the hardware store. It was strange doing all this here back at home.

The people behind the counters were all different and the sights and sounds of her childhood no longer existed. Suddenly she felt old again.

"Hey, we just gonna keep running into each other."

Laura smiled and turned to see her old friend, Grace, walking across the street. "Good morning."

"Morning, girl, you look positively miserable."

"Thanks a lot, I appreciate that."

"I'm messing with you, you know that. But really, what's wrong?"

Laura looked around. "Where is everybody?"

"What do you mean?"

"All our friends are all gone?"

"Some. The others are still here. You remember Judith Clark. Well, she's on the school board so she's around, and Francine Baker is related to the high school principal so she's still around. Betty Green owns the beauty shop across the street and Kelly James is married and living in Elwood."

The names were too familiar. Having gone through her high school yearbook with Tamika the night before started a parade of grinning smiles to flash back at her.

"You know what? I gotta throw a little something this evening to get everyone together. Does anyone else know you're in town?"

"No, I don't think so. You're the only person I recognized."

"And you barely did that, but I ain't mad," Grace joked. "So why don't you stop by my house tonight around seven? I'll tell the girls that I have a surprise."

"Okay," Laura said readily. "Sounds like fun, I can't wait."

"Cool, so I'll see you tonight."

"Wait, where do you live?"

"Same, my mom's house."

"Okay, see you later."

Laura watched Grace sashay across the street in her usual flashy style. She was exactly the same. Bold and audacious, doing exactly what she wanted, when she wanted and to hell with anyone else. Laura always envied that about her.

Anyway, by the time she headed back to the house it was near lunchtime. Tamika was up and dressed and sitting out front on the porch rail talking on the cell phone. She said hi, then when right back to talking.

With the kitchen fully stocked Laura was beginning to feel like her old self again. She wasn't sure if that was a good thing or a bad thing.

"Hey," Tamika said as she walked in and headed for the refrigerator. "Mom, there's a cab pulling up out front. You expecting someone?"

"What, a cab?" she asked rhetorically. "It can't be Aunt Syl. She's not coming until later on in the week," Laura said as she headed to the front door. Tamika followed.

Sylvia Pender, Laura's father's younger sister, was what some might call the black sheep of the family. Now gray-haired and slightly wrinkled with time, she was still totally outrageous.

She'd been staying in the house since her father died three years ago. Keeping her mother company, she stayed even after her mother passed two years ago. Now, with the house so large and the upkeep so strenuous, she was in the process of moving to live closer to her daughter a few miles away.

Sylvia got out of the cab as the driver pulled her small overnight bag from the trunk. She was chuckling and he was laughing outright. She looked up to see Laura and Tamika on the porch coming down the steps. "Hey, how are you, honey child?" she said happily.

The cabdriver placed the small rolling bag on the porch and got back into the cab and drove off still laughing.

"Aunt Sylvia, I thought you weren't coming until later in the week."

"Changed my mind. Come here, honey child, and give me a hug. Lawd, it's been how long?"

"Aunt Syl, I just spoke with you the other day."

"I know but I haven't seen you in forever, not since your mother's funeral. God bless her soul. Girl, what'd you do to yourself?"

"What do you mean?" Laura asked. "I look the same."

"Girl, you lost weight and got buff. Look at you, you look as sharp as a tack."

"Well, that's because I got laid off and started running to relieve stress."

"Well, it's working. You look fantastic. Got me wanting to get up and start running now."

Laura laughed.

"All right, enough of that. Come on over here, missy. Let me see you," Sylvia said to Tamika.

Tamika walked over smiling, bent down and gave her a quick peck on the cheek and a hug. She didn't see her often, but she always liked her aunt Syl. Sylvia was honest and patient and gave mostly everyone and everything a chance.

She listened to all kinds of music and actually liked rap and hip-hop. She once said that rap was nothing but what she'd been doing all her life—telling the truth about what nobody wanted to hear. She was the one relative that Tamika totally related to. Of course, she was also nuts.

"Tamika, girl, you getting just as pretty as you want to

be. Tall and thin, just like your mother. What grade are you in now?"

"I go to eleventh grade in September."

"Eleventh grade already? My, you're getting up there, honey child. So, what are you thinking about doing with your life?"

"I want to take pictures, probably for a magazine or newspaper, or hopefully be a photojournalist."

"A photojournalist?" Tamika nodded. "Oh, that's nice."

Tamika nodded again. "I want to travel all over the world taking pictures."

"You mean of wars and famines and disasters?"

"Well, hopefully I'll be doing photos that are more interesting and not the violent or depressing images," she said.

"Yeah, I can see that," Sylvia said. "You know, you should talk to your mother's friend Grace. Her father's the mayor. Plus he owns the local newspaper. Maybe he could use you this summer."

"You think?" Tamika asked hopefully, glancing at her mother.

"Sure, why not ask? It's only a question. He could say yes or he could say no. Either way, at least you tried."

Tamika paused a moment to consider what her great-aunt said. She was right. If she could get in to talk to Grace's father about taking pictures for his paper, that would be incredible.

"All right, so what are we doing standing out here talking? Let's get inside and get something cool to drink."

"You hungry? I just picked up some groceries," Laura said.

"Nah, I'm just thirsty. What do you have that's tall, dark and cool?" she asked, laughing as she opened the screen door and went inside. Laura followed, shaking her head. Tamika followed after her mother, rolling the small overnight bag behind her. She went upstairs while Sylvia and Laura went into the kitchen. They sat, each with a glass of iced tea, sipping and talking.

"It's so good to see you, Aunt Syl," Laura said, hugging her aunt again just before she sat down.

Sylvia smiled and nodded. "So how's everything going?"

"Not too bad actually," Laura said, nodding happily. "It was a good drive down. We stopped in Arlington to put flowers on Granddad's grave. Then we stopped in Alexandria to the old church."

"The old church graveyard?" Sylvia asked.

Laura nodded.

"How'd Tamika take that? About as well as you did, I'd wager."

"I was okay when Mom took me."

"I beg to differ. You were most definitely freaked out. Took you three weeks to stop complaining about it."

"Well, anyway, Tamika was as expected. It was a shock, granted. How many people see their name etched into a gravestone that dates back a hundred and fifty years ago? She was shaken but she's okay now."

"How's Malcolm?" Sylvia asked.

"He's fine, getting ready to leave for Tokyo again, so all and all everything is just about the same."

"Can't ask for anything more than that, right?" Sylvia said, glancing at her and then looking around the kitchen. "So, when do you want to get started with this place?"

Laura sighed heavily. "I don't know, maybe next week. To tell you the truth, right now I'd like to just chill out. There are so many things going on that I just want to sit back and catch my breath awhile. I ran into Grace. I might give her a call and hang out a bit tonight."

"Good idea."

Laura refilled their drinks and they sat the rest of the afternoon laughing, talking and enjoying memories.

chapter 9

Tamika

A week later Tamika sat out on the front porch with her great-aunt Sylvia, a gray-haired woman with nearly clear skin and a bad case of stiff joints, or so she always said. She walked with a cane on bad days. On good days she still walked with a fancier cane.

As old people go she was at least fun to be with. She had a wicked sense of humor and didn't mind talking about people, even to their faces. She professed to always tell the truth. She said that this late in the game it damn well didn't matter anyway, so you might as well.

It was late evening but not yet dark outside. The moon was high but the sky still had a daylight glow.

"So, how you enjoying your stay so far?" Sylvia asked.

"I'm not," Tamika said truthfully, figuring that her aunt would appreciate her blatant honesty.

"Why not? Sitting around all day on your computer thing, listening to your music with those things stuck in your ears and talking on the phone finally wearing you down?"

Tamika got the biting wit of her sarcasm. "No, it's just boring, nothing to do, that's all. And the reason I do all that is 'cause there's nobody else around."

"And what am I, chopped liver?"

"No, you know what I mean. None of my friends are down here and there's nothing to do."

"Find something else. You keep going on about taking pictures and how much you love it. Well, I ain't seen you take one single picture since I been here and I been here a week now."

"That's 'cause there's nothing to take pictures of."

"Tamika, look around you. Life is all around you, or do you just take pictures of Boston fruit in a bowl?"

"No." Tamika had to smile. She knew that on some level her aunt was right. She hadn't even pulled her camera out of her bag since she arrived a week ago. And any good photographer would have found something to shoot by now.

"So take a picture, then. Go out, find something or somebody."

She nodded and shrugged. "Okay."

The screen door slammed closed. Tamika turned to see her mom standing there, smiling and all dressed up.

"Well, look at you. Don't you look nice," Sylvia said.

"Thanks, Aunt Syl. Well, Tamika, what do you think?"

"You look nice."

"Thanks, sweetie. Okay, I'll be back soon. I don't know what time. I have my cell so call me if you need me."

"Honey child, go on out there and have yourself some fun."

Laura headed down the front steps. "I will. Bye."

Tamika watched as the red car backed up, then drove off. She stared until the last of the red taillights disappeared around the next corner.

"Why is she acting so strange?"

"Strange? How? What do you mean?"

"I mean going out nearly every night and most of the days. It's like she doesn't even want to leave here. She said two weeks. It's already been over a week and she hasn't done anything to get this place started, let alone getting it finished. We're supposed to leave next week. My internship starts then."

"Internship?"

"Yes, it's a photo camp internship. I was supposed to go, but instead I had to be down here to help clean out the house. But like I said, Mom's not even thinking about starting or even doing anything."

"And exactly what have you done since you've been down here? Anything wrong with your hands?"

"No, but it's her job."

"What's her job?"

"To do this, to clean the house out. I don't know what needs to be done."

"And how old are you?" Sylvia asked.

"I mean, I know that things have to be organized and cleaned out, but I don't know what she wants to keep and what needs to be trashed."

"Good point. Why don't you talk to your mother about that?"

"How, when? I can't. She's always hanging out with her friends. It's embarrassing. I'm just glad none of my friends are down here to see this."

"So your mother doesn't hang out at home?"

"No, she works, or rather she worked, then came home and then that was it. She stayed there."

"Sounds pretty boring to me."

Tamika shrugged. "I guess."

Sylvia chuckled. "You guess. Well, honey child, didn't you just tell me that you were bored after one week of just sitting in the house all evening doing nothing? Well, imagine what your mother feels like after how many years."

"But she's got Dad to keep her company."

"Oh, does she?" Sylvia said slyly without giving anything away.

Tamika looked at her. It was obvious she knew more than she was saying. "I guess Dad hangs at the office late most of the time. Then comes home and works some more."

"Uh-huh."

Tamika didn't say anything for some time. She just sat on the wooden rail with her back to the post letting her leg swing. She was thinking about her mother. Maybe she was bored at home too.

"Honey child, Laura's just blowing off a little steam, that's all. Having a bit of fun before she has to go back. I guess sometimes it's hard on her."

"Hard? But she's a parent. She's got the easy part."

"You think being an adult is easy?"

"Yeah," she said quickly.

"How so?"

Tamika starting listing. "No curfew with the car. No school every day whether you like it or not. No drama with teachers. No chores to do every day. Cash on demand any time you want it. Shopping whenever you want."

"Wow, that does sound pretty damn good."

"See...told you, easy."

"Although there's also going to work every day whether you want to or not. Drama with bosses and coworkers. Making beds. Grocery shopping for the family. Cleaning bathrooms. Vacuuming, mortgages, car payments, bank loans."

"Still, Mom's got the life, but she forgot what it was like when she was a teenager."

"Actually it looks like she's starting to catch on."

"But she already did all this hanging out, right?"

"You think so, huh?"

"Yeah."

"Let me enlighten you about your mother's teenage years. She went to school and she went home."

Tamika waited for more, but apparently that's all her aunt was going to say. "So that's it? No partying or hanging out with her friends?"

"Did she ever tell you about her older sister, Debra?"

"Yeah, Aunt Deb, she died before I was born."

"Well, your aunt Deb was five years older than your mother. She thoroughly enjoyed her teen years. She partied and hung out, then eventually dropped out of school and ran away. She died shortly after that. It broke your mother's heart. So by the time Laura was a teenager your grandparents refused to let that happen again. They were extremely strict on her—no parties, no hanging out with friends. She had to go to school, get good grades, then come home and work in the store with them."

"So you're saying that she missed out on her teens, that's why she's doing all this now."

"No, I'm just saying that there's more to your mother than meets the eye. Maybe she is trying to relive her teens, or recapture something she never had. I don't know. I do know that having a little bit of fun won't do nobody no harm, might even do a little good."

"Wait, what about the concert T-shirts in the attic? Mom said they were bought at the concerts, so she must have gone out sometimes. She said they were hers and that she was dancing onstage."

Sylvia looked confused for a second, and then she burst out laughing. "Honey child, I forgot all about those clothes up there. Yeah, oh yeah, she danced onstage all right. I guess it's okay to say something now." She chuckled.

"What do you mean?"

"Your mother used to stay with me once in a while, a long weekend here or there, maybe a week or two weeks at a time in the summer. That's when I lived in Atlanta. So when she was with me we went to concerts, hung out, listened to music and had a ball. Your grandparents never knew about it of course," she said, then winked. "It was our little secret."

"So you snuck her out to have fun," Tamika said.

"Like I said before, a little bit of fun won't do nobody no harm." She yawned, then chuckled again and slapped her bare arm. "All right, that's it for me. I've had it. I'm heading in. These mosquitoes are eating me alive out here." She stood and walked over to the rail. "Good night, Tamika."

"Good night, Aunt Sylvia." They hugged and then Sylvia headed to the screen door to go inside.

Tamika stayed out later. She was thinking about what her aunt had said. She knew that she was at least partly right. There was no reason she couldn't get things started. After all, she was the one who wanted to get back to Boston, not her mom.

When she finally decided to go inside she went up to the attic instead of her bedroom. It was hot upstairs but definitely not as hot as it was the first night she was up there with her mother. Now they kept the ventilation and exhaust fan going all the time.

She turned on the light and looked around. The place was just as they'd left it. There were boxes, opened and closed, all over the floor, and records lying around on the floor beneath the old record player. Tamika went over and started putting things back in boxes. When she got to the journals and diaries she decided to take a peek. After all, it wasn't as if they were new and there was anything interesting. It was just her mother's diary. How interesting could they possibly be?

April 1977

"What am I, blind or something? Deb went to stay with Aunt Syl again. I know she's pregnant. They act like I'm five years old. I'm ELEVEN! I know what pregnant looks like. Imagine that, church folks having a pregnant daughter, boo-hoo. It's not like it never happened before, right? Please. It happens all the time. What's the big deal? Mom's all upset and I think Dad's just shocked. Again, big deal. When Mrs. Evans's daughter down the street got pregnant three years ago everybody was all nice and understanding and everything. But now that it's Deb they're pissed. I don't get it. I hope she has a boy. Anyway, that's all. Bye.

Tamika stopped reading. Her mouth was still open. If it were true and her aunt Deb was pregnant, then what happened to the baby? Tamika turned the page quickly, looking for the next entry.

February 1977

It's my birthday. YEAH!!!! I got a skirt, a pair of jeans and some shirts. Mom and Dad gave me a telescope because I like to look at the stars. It's big and shiny. I went out tonight but the sky was cloudy. I still love it!!! Aunt Syl gave me all these diaries. She said to write in it whenever I feel like screaming no matter if it's something good or something bad. So today I feel like screaming—something good!!!

May 1985
Keith Tyler wrote in my yearbook! I am too pumped. I knew he liked me too. I told Grace—ha! I don't know why she doesn't like him. Hell, half the girls at school have a crush on him but I really love him. I can't wait to talk to him in school tomorrow.

What? Wait... Tamika flipped through a few pages forward then backward. Then she scrambled to look for more diaries dated back before this one, scattering them all over the attic floor. But they were all scrambled up. The dates in the books were out of order and all over the place.

It looked as though when her mother wrote she just grabbed any book and started writing, or maybe this was her way of keeping everybody out since the dates didn't make any sense, the diaries didn't make any sense. Tamika picked up another book and scanned through. It was the same thing. Years, months, days were all mixed up together. It was frustrating to follow any one story line since everything was everywhere and there was no telling when the entries would start or end.

Refusing to be daunted, Tamika persevered. She gathered all the diaries she could find and went back to her bedroom and started reading.

chapter 10

Laura

Laura stretched lazily and sank deeper beneath the covers. Still half-asleep from hanging out the night before with her friends, she was feeling great. It had been about two weeks now and she was still enjoying Fraser, thanks to Grace and her other friends. She lay there awhile longer, then got up halfheartedly, went downstairs and was surprised that Tamika was already up.

"Good morning," Tamika said happily.

"Good morning right back. Wow, look at this spread," Laura said as she checked out the food on the table. Toasted bagels, cream cheese, cheddar cheese, cantaloupe, honeydew, grapes and watermelon covered the kitchen table. She grabbed a piece of melon and bit into it. "Mmm, good, sweet, juicy. So, who did all this, your aunt Sylvia?" she asked, taking a napkin and wiping a drip of juice from her chin as she glanced around the kitchen.

"No, I did it," Tamika said. "Do you want coffee or tea?" she asked with a cup of each in her hand.

"I'll take coffee, thanks," Laura said. "So, what is all this about?"

"We're celebrating," Tamika said happily.

"Really? What are we celebrating?"

"It's been two weeks exactly," Tamika said as soon as her mom sat down at the table.

"What do you mean?" Laura asked as she poured cream into her coffee mug. Thankfully she'd purchased a coffee-maker the second day they'd arrived.

"You said I'd only have to be here for two weeks and then I could go back to Boston for my internship."

"Tamika, look at this place. We're not near about done here. And your father's in Tokyo now. You're not staying at the house alone."

"But you said two weeks."

"I said we'd see how things were going after two weeks. Your father promised you'd be back, not me."

"So that's it? I'm stuck here, then?"

"Is here so bad?"

"Yeah," she said quickly.

"Tamika, give me a break," Laura said.

"This is so wrong."

"Oh, please, don't even think about giving me your drama. You've been here for two weeks. Have you even stepped a foot outside?" she asked. Tamika opened her mouth to respond but was cut off. "Past the front porch?" Laura added. "No, you haven't even given this place a chance, have you? You stay in the house locked in, refusing to go out and even see what Fraser has to offer."

"It has nothing," Tamika said.

"And how would you know that?"

"I checked online."

"Online?" Laura asked.

Tamika nodded.

"Fine, whatever. When this place is finished we'll go, not before."

Tamika walked out. Suddenly she wasn't hungry anymore.

Laura sipped her coffee and decided not to continue the conversation with Tamika. The idea of sending her back had seriously occurred to her. But then a recurrence of the kitchen fire played in the back of her mind. She had grown up since then but she just couldn't take the chance.

"What are you two arguing about this early in the morning?" Sylvia asked as she walked into the kitchen.

"We weren't arguing, we were having a discussion."

"Funny, sounded a whole lot like arguing to me."

"She's pissed as usual."

"Why, what'd you do?"

"Me? I didn't do anything. Why would you think I did something?"

Sylvia sat down and shook her head. "So, what's all this?"

"Tamika's idea of a bribe, I guess. She put this together to remind me that it's been two weeks."

"What's two weeks mean?"

"Her internship starts tomorrow and Malcolm all but promised that she could go back to Boston after two weeks."

"So she wants to leave?" Sylvia asked.

"Yes," Laura said.

Sylvia nodded, understanding. "Maybe you could meet halfway or find a compromise."

"Aunt Syl, there is no halfway. She can't be up there by herself. The last time—"

"Yes, yes, I know, the refrigerator was on fire. But see this from her point of view, from a teenager's point of view. She wants this. She was looking forward to it, right?"

Laura nodded.

"So give her a break."

"Fine," Laura said, standing. "I'm gonna get dressed."

She went upstairs. She stopped at Tamika's bedroom. The door was closed; she knocked and waited for a response.

A few seconds later the door opened and Tamika peeked out.

"Tamika, you can't go back to Boston by yourself."

"Come with me," Tamika said.

"There's still work to do here."

Tamika shrugged. "Okay, fine."

Laura wasn't in the mood to deal with another argument with her daughter, so she just walked away. It was obvious that Tamika wasn't enjoying herself. All she did was stay in her bedroom, play on her computer and talk on the phone. How could that possibly be any fun? Moments later Laura's cell phone rang. It was one of her friends. She decided to deal with Tamika later.

chapter 11

Tamika

BEING pissed off seemed to be the order of the day, so Tamika just went with it. It had been two weeks and it was obvious that they weren't leaving. She heard her mother laughing and talking on the phone down the hall. Obviously she was having a good old time. Tamika picked up a diary and started reading again.

Since she used to like puzzles when she was younger, Tamika started putting the diary dates back to rights as best she could. It had become a kind of mission for her. There was still no real understanding to the order, but at least she was able to find some sequence of events. And since her mother apparently only wrote in the diaries when, as instructed by Aunt Sylvia on her tenth birthday, she felt like screaming, the entries only detailed good things or bad things.

October 1983
I want to get my ears pierced again. What's the big deal? Everybody has at least two or three holes in their ear-

lobes except me. It's not like I'm asking for a tattoo or something crazy like that. By the way, Deb has a tattoo of a heart on her hip. Mom and Dad don't even know.

September 1981
Today is the first day of school. High school, I forgot how much I hate this place, same stupid people, same stupid stuff. Everybody hates me but that's okay because I hate them too. I hate this place. I can't wait to leave. Thank God for Grace!!

June 1985
Keith is an ASSHOLE! He wrote the same thing in every girl's yearbook. JERK!!!

December 1985
I stayed over with Aunt Syl for Christmas. We went to two concerts. I'm so glad that her new boyfriend works for the radio station and a record label. He gets all kinds of cool tickets. I am totally coming back here next month. Prince is coming!!!

April 1983
He asked me to tutor him! YEAH!!!

August 1978
It's HOT as HELL! Deb had a girl. YEAH, I'm an auntie!!

October 1981
Does it look like we have money? Yeah, we live in the biggest house on the block and the stupid town is

named after somebody in my family from way back, but that don't mean we have a ton of money. Anyway, Deb is in trouble. She stayed out all night and decided to drop out of school. Mom and Dad are pissed off.

November 1981

Shit!!! In American history class today we studied the history of our town. Like I need a history lesson to tell me that, I hear it all the time. My grandmother tells me every other day. So of course I have to hear what I heard all my life in school. All about my slave ancestor who screwed some old white guy and got pregnant. General Joseph Fraser was a jerk. I hate this place.

March 1982

Deb is in trouble again but instead of taking it out on her I get punished. All I want to do is go over to Grace's house for her sleepover. But NO, I can't go because Deb is in trouble and I MIGHT get in trouble too. I hate her sometimes. When I have kids I'm never gonna live here. I'm gonna move as far away from this place as I can and NEVER, NEVER, EVER come back. Then I'm gonna let my kids do exactly what they want to do no matter what it is.

August 1982

The shit hit the fan and Deb is in serious trouble. What is wrong with her???

September 1982

Since I spent most of the summer with Aunt Syl in Atlanta, I missed everything going on around here. Grace permed her hair and left it on too long. Then her mother made her go to her friend in Elwood to get most of it cut off because most of it fell out anyway.

October 1982
I cut my hair in solidarity, HA! Yeah, me!!! They hate it but I LOVE it!!!

October 1985
As usual, I spent the morning sitting beside Keith. I swear he's perfect. Grace still thinks I'm crazy. She thinks I like him. I lied and told her that I'm all over him but really I'm not.

December 1985
My aunt Syl picked me up this weekend. I hope we have fun at her place. I love going there. At least she lets me do things.

March 1977
Sometimes I hate my sister. Debra is so selfish and my parents let her do anything she wants. Right now she gets to hang out with her friends and I can't go with her. I hate this place.

September 1977
Debra was visiting her friend but now she's not coming back. Mom and Dad are all upset. Aunt Syl came over last night.

December 1983
I saw Keith over Christmas vacation. I know I can't be-

lieve it myself. I was so shocked. We were in the mall looking for something to give my dad for Xmas and I looked out the store window and there he was just standing there. It was weird and scary because I saw him in Atlanta.

There was something strange about reading her mother's teenage diary, and even though all the entries were all scrambled she still got a pretty good sense of what her mother was like when she was a teenager. Aunt Syl was right. She apparently didn't have much of a teen life. She was overprotected and sheltered and the only fun she seemed to have was with Aunt Syl.

Tamika tried putting the entries in some kind of a chronological order, but it still didn't seem to work. After reading a few more entries she recognized a familiar admission from one she had read earlier. It was about what her mother wanted to do when she had children.

May 1983
I still can't believe I'm an aunt. Deb's little girl is so sweet. I want to be just like Aunt Sylvia. Or even better, I want to be a fun mom when I grow up and have kids. Maybe I'll have a daughter and name her Tamika. But either way I'm never gonna live here in Fraser. I'm moving as far away from this place as I can and NEVER, NEVER, EVER coming back. Then I'm gonna let my kids do exactly what they want to do no matter what it is.

Tamika lay back and wondered what had happened between then and now. The heat of the day made her sleepy.

She lay down and closed her eyes, continuing to consider her mother's diaries. Moments later she fell asleep. When she woke up there was a note on her bed. Aunt Sylvia had gone out visiting and her mother had gone out and wouldn't be back until late. She ate, checked out her MySpace, watched television, then went back to sleep.

chapter 12

Laura

"Good morning, sleepyhead," Laura said, then paused for a response. "Good morning," she repeated. "Come on, time to get up, rise and shine."

Hearing her, Tamika didn't move, of course, as an uninvited voice sang out, breaking the constant chatter of morning birds.

"Hey, good morning in there."

Tamika opened one eye, groaned, then rolled over and covered her head with the floral top sheet, but the bright sun streamed through the cotton anyway. She grabbed and held tight just as the room brightened even more. Hearing her mother rip the curtains open, she grabbed a pillow and covered her head, then groaned again.

"Good morning," Laura repeated.

"Morning," Tamika groaned.

"Are you ready to get your day started?"

"What time is it?" Tamika muttered.

"Ten-thirty," Laura said in that chipper way she did as she sat down on the side of the bed.

"Ten-thirty in the morning?"

"Of course in the morning. Come on, time to get up. The sooner we get started, the sooner we'll be done. I need to run out for an hour or so this morning. I have a list of things I need to pick up so come on, get up and get started. I made breakfast."

As if she hadn't just heard what her mother said, Tamika only focused on the time. "It's ten-thirty in the morning."

"Yes, it is."

"Wait, you cooked breakfast?" Tamika said.

"Yes, I cooked breakfast."

"Where's Aunt Syl?"

"Aunt Syl decided to go visit a friend."

"Another sick friend? How many sick friends does she have and what does she do, make house calls or something? For real, everybody she knows is sick. What's up with that? Don't you think that's strange?" Tamika asked.

Laura never said that her aunt's friend was sick and she didn't correct Tamika's wrong assumption either.

"She'll be back probably tomorrow. So I thought it would be nice to have breakfast together for a change. We've been here awhile now, so I thought I'd do something a little special. Now come on before the food gets cold. You need a full stomach. We have a lot to do today."

"Mom, the last time you cooked breakfast for me I was in elementary school."

"Correction. That was the last time you ate a breakfast I cooked. I've cooked breakfast, you just refused to eat, running out of the house every morning like the place was on fire."

"That's 'cause I eat at school," Tamika said as she finally sat up and opened both eyes.

"Never mind about that. Come on, get up. I'm pouring pancakes in five minutes."

"Carbs?"

"Yes, carbs. Get your butt up and come on downstairs," she said, then stood up. "By the way, I spoke to Aunt Syl before she left this morning. She told me that you were ready to get started getting this place cleared out."

"She told you that?" Tamika asked.

"Yes, I think it's a good idea. Maybe we should start taking care of business, which is why I'm headed out after breakfast to pick up some packing supplies."

"Is that all she said?" Tamika asked.

"Yes, why? Is there more I need to know?"

"No, nothing. We were just talking about growing up and mosquitoes the other night."

"Mosquitoes?"

"Yes, we might need to pick up some outdoor spray."

"All right, come on, then, let's get started. Breakfast is in ten minutes."

Of course getting her daughter downstairs took much longer than the ten minutes she allotted her. A fifteen-minute shower and another fifteen minutes to dress and primp finally brought Tamika to the kitchen table.

Forty-five minutes later, after a surprisingly leisurely breakfast with her daughter where they discussed packing up, Laura got in the car, slid the roof back and drove off. She reached over and found a radio station she used to listen to years ago. They just happened to be playing the same Chris Brown song she'd heard driving into town a couple of weeks ago. She started laughing and singing along.

With her list in hand she started checking off stops each time she picked up supplies. Boxes, tape, bubble wrap, markers and more boxes. Next to the hardware store was a cute little clothing boutique.

Laura stood at the front window admiring the fashions. In a reflection behind her she saw two teens walk by in a slow, carefree, lackadaisical cadence. They were talking happily as they went inside. One tall and thin, the other shorter and heavier, they reminded her of Tamika and her friend Lisa.

Her thoughts immediately went to her daughter and then to their drive into town. Singing happily, then in the attic looking at old photos, they had had a great time and really connected. Tamika's sullen mood seemed to ease away and she was a joy to be with. Earlier she'd been so different. She was at her wits' end with her daughter and just didn't know what to do about her anymore. It seemed that lately they were living in two different worlds.

She walked into the store and looked around. Perfect.

She picked up a cute top for Tamika, then decided to get one for herself. She tried it on and decided to wear it. She also added sunglasses and then grabbed a huge straw hat. She walked out wearing her new purchases and feeling fantastic.

Just as she loaded everything in the car's trunk her cell rang. She grabbed it and answered without checking the caller ID. "Hello."

"Hey, finally. We've been playing phone tag for so long I figured you didn't want to talk to me."

"My cell's been crazy. I think I need a new battery."

"So, how's it going?" Malcolm asked.

"Great, how's it going with you?" Laura answered.

"Good. We basically work real late and then I grab something to eat, then pass out. I forgot how crazy this place is."

"Crazy, huh?" she said, sitting behind the wheel and looking around her.

"Too crazy."

"So what time is it there?"

"Um, I don't really know. My watch is still set on Boston time. I guess I'd better change that, huh?"

"Yeah, I guess you better."

"So how's it going there?" he asked.

"Slowly," she said. "I'm out getting boxes today."

He replied but she barely heard every other word. "Malcolm, the phone's crazy again. Let me call you back."

"Okay, call me later. I love you," he said.

"Bye." Laura closed the cell. She wasn't sure why she didn't return his endearment; she just didn't.

Sitting in a bright red convertible car with her wide-brim straw hat and dark shades on, she looked like the only Hollywood star. Residents passed by and stared, not recognizing her and not sure if they should recognize her, so they just stared slyly or boldly gawked. Then a big old truck swung a U-turn and pulled up beside her. Laura glanced over and up at the driver.

"Hey, lady of leisure, how's it going?"

Laura smiled. Hearing her friend's voice was exactly what she needed. "Let's see. I've been unemployed for six months having worked at the same advertising agency since my junior year in college. My husband is in Japan with a woman he had an affair with and my daughter's nuts."

"Oh, good. Nothing's changed since last night. Sounds like you need a drink."

"A bit early for that, isn't it?" Laura asked.

"Not at all. I need some serious caffeine. Follow me."

Laura smiled, nodded and started the engine. She followed the big old truck as it bumped and jarred down the uneven street, then stopped in front of a coffeehouse and bakery.

This used to be their favorite hangout. While the cool kids hung at the movies in Elwood, Grace and Laura and their friends hung here at Mrs. Oliver's Bakery.

"Perfect place. I can't believe it's still around."

"Oh, it's still here. Changed hands about a dozen times but it's still here. Never the same, funny that."

"I don't care. It's just nice to see the old sign still hanging up there."

"Girl, this thing is too hot."

"It's a rental, you know."

"Get out, where's your car?"

"Know what? Somehow I just didn't feel like driving a mommy minivan over a thousand miles."

"I don't blame you, honey, this thing says something. Come on, if I don't get some caffeine in me I'm gonna pass out. I swear I don't know what I was thinking hanging out with you like I'm nineteen again."

"There's nothing wrong with that. If I remember correctly, nineteen wasn't bad at all and neither was last night."

They laughed, enjoying the moment. At nineteen, both had come back from their first year at college and nearly torn the small town of Fraser apart. "Think they're ready for us again?" Laura asked.

"Hell no. They still trying to clean up from behind us last time."

They laughed again, loud and hard. Laura shook her head, enjoying the freedom of just hanging out with her friend.

"Man, those were the days," Grace said, still chuckling. "But listen, what are you doing for the Fourth?"

"Nothing, why?"

"I'm having a little July Fourth backyard cookout. Nothing major, just a little something something to pass the time. Why don't you and Tamika stop by? Judith and Francine are coming and I invited some of our old friends. I know they'd love to see you. It's my birthday celebration too and I'm bringing it in style."

"Wait, your birthday's on the Fourth?" Laura asked, slightly embarrassed that she didn't remember. "No, wait a minute. I know my memory can't be that bad. If I'm not mistaken your birthday is a month after mine, which makes it four months ago."

"Girl, every day is my birthday now. It's a short life, so celebrate as often and as much as you can. That's what I say."

Laura chuckled. "Okay, can't argue with that. Sounds good to me. The old gang, huh? So you still see everybody?"

"Not everybody, but some," Grace said.

"But you know, on second thought, I've got a ton of things to do. It's been two weeks and I haven't even started going through the house yet," Laura said, ready to make her apologies, and then it occurred to her that this was exactly what she needed. "No, you know what? Yes, I'll be there. What time?"

"Party starts any time after one. Food goes down at twelve-thirty so act accordingly. You know ain't nobody shy around here when it comes to grubbing on some grilled food."

"What should I bring?" Laura asked.

"Just bring yourself and Tamika, that's all."

"What about food, snacks, soda?"

"If you want something special, fine, bring it along. We'll already have the usual staples there—hot dogs, chicken, hamburgers, ribs, all kinds of salads and stuff."

Just then a dark car drove by slowly. The windows were

open and the driver turned to them and nodded as he passed. By the time the car drove farther down the block, Laura's mouth was wide open.

"Was that...?"

"Uh-huh."

"And did he just...?"

"Uh-huh."

"Keith Tyler," Laura just about whispered as she remembered her dream from a week earlier. "I didn't know he was still around town."

"Oh yeah, he's a major player around here now. He was in Dallas for a while. Then when his dad died and left him the business he came back. I think he travels between here and Texas a couple times a month. Apparently he has a business in both places."

"Really?" Laura said.

"Uh-huh. Brother used to have deep pockets. I don't know about now. I hear he's struggling for every penny big-time. Too many investments, forgetting to pay Uncle Sam, you know the deal. Now he's just trying to hold on to anything, at least that's what they say."

"Really?" Laura repeated.

"Hell, I'm surprised he hasn't stopped by to see you."

"For what? It's not like the man even spoke to me back in the day except for when I tutored him."

"Real estate, girl. You're selling that big old house so you know he's gonna want a piece of that, plus all the history stored up in there."

"What?"

"Oh yeah, he's big-time in real estate, investments, equity and foreclosure recovery business. Though I heard that you gotta keep an eye on him, 'cause the man is too slick with his contract mumbo jumbo. He even had the feds on his case a while back, but they couldn't prove anything. It was in the paper for weeks. Apparently he was accused of defrauding a few women and taking their money. Their houses foreclosed and the equity disappeared into thin air. So don't be surprised if he steps your way."

"The man doesn't even know I exist."

"Times change," Grace said as she noticed Laura still looking down the street. "You know he's still single. And if I remember correctly you had a serious crush on him. Maybe you should get a little something something for good ol' times while you're here. If I remember correctly the man still owes you. I still can't believe you tutored him all of tenth grade for free when his dad was loaded."

"Don't think so. And as you said, times change." She shrugged. "I have a husband at home in Boston, or rather in Tokyo."

"What did you tell me he was doing there again?"

"He's an engineer and a construction manager. His company is doing a trade job over there."

"Cool," Grace said.

"Not really," Laura said, changing her demeanor.

"Now, that definitely sounds like drama, girl."

"You know how it is—married for umpteen years, bored for umpteen-plus."

"Sounds like my ex. He bored himself into three affairs that I knew about."

Laura just shook her head. "Heard that."

"The only good thing about my marriage was my two sons."

"You're divorced now, right?"

"Lordy, yes. The man was driving me crazy with his stupid shit. I had to let his ass go," she said as they laughed.

"I'm single and going wild. After I hit forty I decided that it was all about me. I was tired of my kids giving me drama. All I'm about now is having fun, ginger ale and having more fun."

Laura smiled wishfully. She knew that Grace had started having children early, so her kids were basically already grown. She could afford to have fun and chill. "Sounds like heaven."

"You know I do my thing," Grace said, popping her shoulders and dancing in her seat.

"I was just telling Tamika about us dancing onstage."

"Oh Lordy, I forgot all about that time. Now, that was a night, wasn't it?"

"It sure was. I swear it was that T-shirt I bought that got me up there," Laura said.

"Whatever it was, you were too much. I never saw you so free and having so much fun."

Laura nodded as Grace continued talking about that night and others. But all Laura could think about was wearing that T-shirt and being free.

"Lordy, girl, I can't be sitting here talking to you all day. I've got work to do and a party to finish putting together."

"Yeah, me too. I have a house to empty out and a trunkful of boxes and bubble wrap."

"Okay, now don't forget, one o'clock," Grace said as she stood and started to head back to her truck.

"I won't. See you later," Laura said, deciding to stick around awhile longer and check out the town before going back to the house and whatever new drama was probably waiting for her there.

She sipped her coffee and just sat chilling out.

"Laura, is that you? I heard you were back in town."

She turned around and shaded her eyes as the sun blinded

her momentarily. She could have sworn she saw who she knew she couldn't have.

"Okay, you gonna act like you don't remember me, right? You got me through tenth grade history class, right?"

"Keith? Keith Tyler?"

He nodded. "Have I changed that much?" he asked.

Damn, he looked just as good as he did over twenty years ago—big, strong and handsome. Mocha brown with bedroom eyes that promised the world, he looked every bit of what she had expected. He'd shaved his head and it looked damn good on him.

"No, really, I'm just surprised that you…" she said, then paused. "Never mind. Hi, how are you?" She held her hand out to shake, but instead he pulled her up out of her seat and enveloped her in an all-too-friendly embrace. "Hi," she said breathlessly when he finally chose to release her.

"Look at you. You are…" he said, then paused and let his eyes roam the contours of her body. "Looking fine sitting here all Hollywood." She blushed and looked away. "Seriously, you look incredible." He licked his lips slowly as his eyes continued to roam over every inch of her body.

"It's good to see you too, Keith. How've you been?"

"You know, I'm just handling my business. May I join you?" he asked of the empty seat beside her.

She nodded. "Sure, um, I thought I heard that you were in Texas," she said as he moved the chair to sit closer to her.

"Yeah, I was, but then I decided to come back here. My dad passed and I took over his business."

"Oh, I'm sorry to hear that. I remember him. He was a nice man."

Keith nodded. "So, what are you doing now?"

"Just chillin'," she said as hip as she could.

His cell rang. He grabbed it and looked at the number.

"So, what are you doing in town?" he probed more.

"I have to take care of some business."

"Oh," he said, smiling, nodding and licking his full lips lazily in the way that he always did that turned her sixteen-year-old stomach to mush. "Nothing too distracting, I hope."

"No, just family business."

He nodded. "How long?"

"I don't know yet, it depends. Why?"

"Well, I'd like to see you, maybe catch up. So if you don't have any other plans this evening, how about dinner tonight?"

"Sorry, I do have plans this evening."

"Change them," he nearly ordered in all seriousness as his cell phone rang again and he checked the number.

"No, I can't. Sorry."

"Tomorrow, then," he suggested.

"It's a holiday and I already have plans."

He shook his head slowly and licked his lips again. Laura's heart thundered in her chest. This man, Keith Tyler, was the catchall through high school. Of course he barely even spoke to her. She wasn't in his circle. He was a football player and hung with the cool kids. She was just a regular student, easily ignored and easily discarded. Funny how things changed.

"Come on, one dinner."

"Sorry, anyway…" she said, then smiled, unbelieving.

"What?" he asked.

"Nothing, forget it."

"No, what? Tell me."

"I was just going to say that I'm just surprised that you even remembered my name."

"Why would you say that?" he asked, seemingly affronted by her remark.

"Because in high school you barely even spoke to me. We didn't exactly hang out in the same crowd."

"No," he denied with shock, "that can't be right. Are you sure about that?"

"Oh yes," she affirmed.

"No, really?"

She nodded. He smiled the classic smile that always made her body tingle. "My bad. I guess I missed out on something really special." His eyes deepened their effect on her. "Well, I guess I'll have to make up for lost time."

"Don't worry about it."

"So, family business, huh?"

"Yes, I'm clearing out my parents' home."

He smiled, cracking a serious dimple in his cheek. "Oh yeah, I remember that house. Diamond Point Road. Huge, right?"

She nodded.

"Man, I always wanted to see the inside of that place."

"Really?" she asked, wondering if he was sincere.

"Oh yeah, it was the cornerstone of the neighborhood— of the town really."

"All that, huh?"

"Oh yeah, all that."

This time Laura's cell rang and she answered. It was her aunt Sylvia talking a mile a minute. "Aunt Syl, wait. Hold on a minute," she said, then mouthed to Keith, "I gotta take this." He nodded. "Okay, okay, yeah, okay," she said, then repeated but wasn't paying any attention. She was too busy watching Keith.

"Aunt Syl, let me call you right back, okay?" She looked up in time to see Keith glance back at her, smiling as she closed her cell. "I gotta go."

He nodded wordlessly.

She grabbed her purse and sunglasses from the tabletop. "See you later maybe," she said.

He nodded again. "Most definitely." His brow arched as he wet his lips.

Laura stood, replaced her dark sunglasses, then walked over to the bright red convertible car. For the first time in a long while she was too proud of herself. She got in and drove away with a quick wave, seeing him standing watching her from the rearview mirror. The exit would have totally missed had she gotten into her usual soccer-mom minivan.

chapter 13

Tamika

After breakfast with her mother, Tamika staggered back to her bedroom window and watched her mother drive off down the street. The top was down and she could tell that it was already hot outside. She stood at the screened window hoping for a breeze. None came so she went back over and plopped back down on the bed. The ceiling fan spun around but only blew warm air around the room. She grabbed a pillow and held it over her face, then fell back and screamed. There was no way she was going to survive here for much longer.

Later, as per the conversation with her aunt and then with her mother, Tamika decided to go up to the attic and get started going through some of the boxes. It was dusty and old and smelly, but it was also kind of cool up there, though she'd never openly admit it.

She spent the morning and afternoon in the attic. Digging through decades- and sometimes centuries-old memories was more exciting than she had thought.

She sat at an old rolltop desk and started going through

the drawers. She found a pair of wire-rimmed eyeglasses and put them on. She could barely see. "Dang, they must have been half-blind," she said, then took them off and continued rummaging through the drawers. In the next drawer she found some old stamps and a few coins dating back to the twenties and thirties. She found letters wrapped with a white ribbon and two fountain pens. The next few drawers were filled with lots of books with copyrights from the last two centuries. She also found more letters, a few journals and some old leather-bound ledgers that dated back over one hundred and fifty years ago or more.

Opening and flipping through the pages and reading the written notations, she was amazed by the historical references. Within the ledger were more letters. She read them, then held them aside.

Selecting some of the more interesting letters and ledgers, she decided that she'd talk to her mother about taking them to be appraised. She set them aside to take pictures of everything just in case.

Continuing, she found a crystal and pewter inkwell and silver makeup and cigarette case with an engraving dating back to the twenties. She also found a couple of small beaded purses and some hair combs and a jewelry box containing dozens of colorful trinkets that looked like new.

After thoroughly checking out the attic and going through all of the boxes and relabeling them, she decided to do something different and check out the basement. It definitely wasn't as interesting as the attic. There was mostly old furniture and a few paintings, rugs and lots of old books. She took a few photos, but not finding much of interest she grabbed her hoard of booty from the attic and went to her bedroom to her laptop.

Curiously she went online and tried to do some research on some of the things she found. Unable to get much information, she decided to try again later. In the meantime she checked her MySpace. Surprisingly, Sean had responded to her last post. She was just about to write something back when her cell rang. It was Lisa.

"Hey, what's up?" Lisa said happily.

"Don't ask. Apparently my sentence here has been extended."

"You gotta stay longer, huh?"

"Yep. I think my mom's having too much fun to even want to think about leaving. For the last two weeks she's been hanging out like crazy, dressing like she's a teenager and she even got highlights in her hair now."

"What kind of highlights? Where?"

"All over. They actually look nice but I don't want to talk about that. What's up with you?"

"Girl, wait till you hear…" Lisa went on to tell Tamika about the latest in Boston, which included Drea being pregnant and Lexea's parents just up and moving away.

"For real?" Tamika said, smiling.

"For real, I heard that Lexea knew she was moving way back in April but didn't say anything to anybody. Since they were renting they just moved, like, overnight. I have no idea what's up with that."

"That's a trip."

"Yep, and about Drea, she actually has a little bump and everything. Word is the father is some old guy she was hanging with that her parents hated. Anyway, they say she was trying to get married but it's all up in the air right now. I even heard that he was already married."

"For real," Tamika said, not at all surprised.

"Oh, and get this. Guess who stopped by the store yesterday."

"Who?"

"Justin, talkin' 'bout where Tamika at."

"What?"

"Yep, so I told him that truthfully I had no idea. 'Cause for real I don't know where Fraser is, so it's not like I was lying or anything. Anyway, he was like, he stopped by your house a few times and there was nobody home," Lisa said in just about one sentence and one breath. Tamika chuckled. "So if you want him back I guess you can have him. He said that if I heard from you to ask you to call him."

"Call him?"

"Yeah, you gonna call?"

"You know what, I've been down here for, like, two weeks and I haven't even thought about him once until you just said his name. And like I said before, I'm tired of his stupid stuff."

"I hear you. The last thing you need is more drama. So, what are you doing down there all day?"

"On the computer mostly, but guess what. You would not believe all the stuff I just found in the attic and in the basement here. It's like an antique warehouse in this place."

"For real? See, told you," Lisa said. "What do you think they're all worth?"

"I don't know. I tried to find some of this stuff on eBay, but that didn't exactly work so I guess I have to get my mom to get it appraised someplace. But for real, it's old, old. It's gotta be worth something."

"I knew it. So, what'd you find?"

"Okay, first in the attic there's this huge rolltop desk like in the old movies and it has all these drawers and secret compartments. I found some old money."

"Money, like in cash money?"

"No, coins. Like dimes, quarters and nickels. They're old and dated in the twenties and thirties and even before that, like before the turn of the century—the last century. But there are also some huge pennies like the size of half dollars but they're brown like pennies. The dates are rubbed off."

"Well, maybe they can check it some other way."

"I don't know, maybe. I also found stamps and some eyeglasses. Then it has these secret compartments and I found some books with stamps in them like for stamp collecting. They have all kinds of stamps inside."

"That sounds promising."

"Yeah, maybe. Then in this other compartment I found all these really cool letters wrapped in ribbon. They were in the envelopes and most of them were postmarked in the 1920s."

"The 1920s, for real?"

"Yeah, they were love letters."

"For real? Cool."

"Yeah, I'll bring 'em back so you can read them."

"Who were they from?"

"I don't know, somebody. But wait, these other letters I found in these seriously old ledgers were dated back to the 1870s. That General Fraser I told you about before, well, I think that he was having some kind of argument with his family. 'Cause some of the letters are all about him having his own life away from them."

"That's the guy that owned your ancestors, right?"

"Yeah, I think."

"This is so cool. How many people can actually say they have a town named after them?"

"The ledgers are records of the slaves his family owned and papers of freedom."

"That's for-real museum stuff. You gotta get that stuff appraised. What else?"

"Okay, then I went down to the basement. There's all this seriously old furniture down there and boxes of dishes and tons of books and paintings. It's like another whole houseful of furniture down there."

"Is the stuff old and antique too?"

"Nah, I don't think so. I think most of it's more like retro back to the fifties or the sixties. There's an old radio and this weird two-sided toaster and even a black-and-white television."

"Do they work?"

"I don't know, I didn't try it."

Lisa laughed. "I wonder if you'd see all those old black-and-white programs like *The Lone Ranger*."

"Lisa, you do know that the shows aren't in there, right? I guess if I plugged it in I'd get whatever's on TV nowadays, except no cable."

"Still, that stuff might be worth something. You never know. Definitely check it out."

"Yeah, I will. I started taking pictures of everything just in case they want to see some of the pieces."

"Good idea."

"I just gotta find a place to take it."

"Go online."

"Good idea."

The conversation continued as Lisa told Tamika that her mother was coming in mid-July to get her and that she couldn't wait.

"You're so lucky that your mom's so cool," Tamika said.

"What makes you think she's cool?"

"Because she lets you do things you want to do."

"That's only when I'm visiting her. I remember when my parents were married. They argued all the time and neither one let me do anything. When they broke up they loosened up on me. To tell you the truth, I don't know if I like the trade-in."

Tamika thought about her parents. Like Lisa, their breaking up to get freedom wasn't a trade-in she wanted either. "So what else is happening around the way?" she asked.

Lisa told her about Justin's latest party. Tamika seriously wasn't interested. But it was a flop anyway, so no big deal.

"How's Sean?" Lisa asked.

"I don't know. He said that he was coming down on the Fourth but I haven't heard anything yet."

"The Fourth—that's tomorrow."

"Yeah, I know."

Lisa sighed heavily. "I can't believe how fast summer is going."

"Yeah, me either," Tamika said.

"Listen, I gotta get ready to go to work. I'll call you when I go on my break," Lisa said.

"Okay, see ya."

Tamika hung up thinking about Justin. It was the first time since the party the last day of school. It seemed funny now. They'd hung out all of ninth grade and most of tenth grade, but all that was getting tired and somewhere along the way their interests changed. Either way, she wasn't all broken up, and that should say something.

She went back online and immediately got an IM.

Sean: hey, R U there?
Tamika: yep
Sean: how u been?
Tamika: okay, U

Sean: working hard
Tamika: where?
Sean: @ the state park
Tamika: u like it?
Sean: $$'s okay, how do U like Fraser?
Tamika: haven't seen it yet
Sean: y not?
Sean: u gotta get out
Tamika: waiting 4 U
Sean: cool, I'll give U a tour
Tamika: promise?
Sean: yeah. what R U doing on the 4th?
Tamika: IDK—Y?
Sean: that's when I'm coming down.

Tamika looked at his response. She wasn't sure if she was happy or what. It just hung there. She finally responded.

Tamika: ok
Sean: there's a big fair, parade & celebration
Tamika: N Fraser?

She typed, wondering why she hadn't heard anything about it yet.

Sean: no, N the next town over
Tamika: okay
Sean: that's where my grandparents live
Tamika: how's Boston?
Sean: I saw U'R boy
Tamika: who?
Sean: Justin

Of course Tamika knew exactly who he was talking about, but it was strange as she told Lisa that she hadn't thought about him since she left home.

Tamika: that's nice
Sean: I thought U 2 were tight
Tamika: we decided 2 chill
Sean: good idea
Tamika: u think?
Sean: DEFINITELY!!
Tamika: me 2
Sean: I saw the pictures U put on U'R MySpace—NICE
Tamika: thanx
Sean: cemetery?
Tamika: Yeah, whatever—don't ask
Sean: Goth?
Tamika: my mom's idea
Sean: what's the story?
Tamika: long & boring
Tamika: I'll tell you L8R
Sean: promise?
Tamika: yeah.
Tamika: I gotta go
Sean: take more pictures, I like seeing 'em
Tamika: okay, bye

chapter 14

Laura

The Fourth of July came in with a bang. So, to say that it was just another holiday backyard picnic party would be grossly understating the event held at Grace's house. First of all, nearly everybody in town showed up. The backyard, front yard, porch and decks were packed. Smoke from the massive grills hovered all around as dozens, maybe hundreds of people hung out having a blast.

The adults danced, joked around, played cards, screamed, yelled and argued, then played some more. Smaller kids ran around chasing each other, bumping into everybody. Others played badminton or just sat out in lawn chairs in sunglasses and slept.

Ribs, hot dogs, hamburgers and chicken cooked on the grills constantly. Salads of all kinds sat in the cooler along with chips, dips, vegetables and sodas. Grace was celebrating her birthday again and she was, as usual, doing it in style. As she said, "It's not every day you turn forty, but it's every day you can celebrate it."

Laura wholeheartedly agreed.

She'd been partying and helping Grace celebrate since the minute she arrived in town. The food was off-the-chain delicious and the music was real music, from-her-day music, and she was laughing, dancing and having a good old time.

"Girl, look at you, just taking over the dance floor," Grace said when she danced up beside Laura. "Reminds you of the good old days, don't it?" They bumped, closed fists, then hips, then burst out laughing.

When the song ended Laura walked over and plopped down on the bench next to Tamika, who had been sitting texting. She exhaustedly fanned herself with her fingers. Tamika closed her phone when Laura sat down.

"Hey, sweetie, how you doing?"

"Fine," Tamika said uneasily.

"Having a good time?"

"Not really. This is your crowd, remember?"

"There're some teenagers around here," Laura said, looking around but not seeing anyone under the age of twenty-five.

"Mom, they left ten minutes after they got here and that was four hours ago."

"Well, you can still have a good time, can't you?" Laura asked.

"No, not really," Tamika said.

"Well, did you at least get something to eat?"

"Yeah, it was good," she said. "So, when are we leaving? Soon?"

Before Laura could answer she looked up beyond Tamika to see Keith Tyler walking toward her. She smiled. "Hey."

"Hey, we meet again," he said smoothly.

"I didn't know you were coming here today."

"I decided at the last minute to crash. So this is why you stood me up," he said.

Tamika turned and looked up at him, then to her mother. The words "stood me up" obviously implied that they had had a planned date.

"I didn't stand you up, 'cause we didn't have a date."

"All right, you got me there. So who's this, your daughter?"

"Yes. Tamika, this is an old friend, Keith Tyler. Keith, my daughter, Tamika."

Tamika nodded as he swallowed her hand in his large one and shook. "Nice to meet you, Tamika. Are you having a good time?"

Laura looked at her sternly, expecting her to be as truthful as she was to her. But instead Tamika smiled politely and nodded. "It's okay."

"Yeah, I get the picture. Not exactly a party at Diddy's place."

"You know him?" she asked skeptically.

"Oh yeah," he said, obviously wanting to impress her. "He and I go way back. As a matter of fact, I was just at his place in the Hamptons a few weeks ago. He had a nice little gathering up there, a lot of big names. He's talking about having his annual white party at his Long Island home this year."

"His white party, huh?" Tamika said.

"By invitation only, and when it reads white he means white, only white, nothing but bleached-to-the-bone white. So heads-up, don't be steppin' up in there with no cream, eggshell or ecru, 'cause he will sure nuff bump your behind out of there."

Laura laughed but Tamika wasn't impressed. She could have found out the same information on Google. "Uh-huh," Tamika said, not really buying it.

"Listen, I brought my daughter with me, much to her complaining the whole drive over here."

"You have a daughter?" Laura asked.

"Yes," he said. "Listen, why don't I introduce you to her, Tamika? I'm sure she'd like to talk to someone closer to her own age." He looked around, then toward a young girl standing on the back porch talking to the man playing the music. He beckoned to her and she walked over only half smiling.

"You want me?" she said, standing by his side.

"Laura, Tamika, this is my daughter, Jaleesa. Jaleesa, this is Laura and her daughter, Tamika."

"Hi," Jaleesa said.

"See," Keith said, speaking to his daughter, "I told ya you wouldn't be the only person under the age of twenty here."

Jaleesa smirked without answering.

"So, why don't you and Tamika chat while I have the next dance with this lovely young lady, Laura?" He held out his hand and pointed Laura toward the dance area. She went willingly.

Jaleesa sucked her teeth and rolled her eyes. "My dad's a trip. He thinks he's such a player. I hope your mom's not falling for his crap. So, where y'all from? I know y'all ain't from no place around here."

"Boston, Massachusetts," Tamika said. She could tell that Jaleesa was a lot younger than she was. "Actually, just outside of Boston."

"For real," Jaleesa said excitedly. "I was thinking about going to either MIT in Cambridge or to the University of Massachusetts in Boston. How is it up there? They say the winters are brutal. But I really don't care as long as I'm away from here. You are so lucky. You get to go home away from all this."

"Boston's okay. I had a college tour at the University of Massachusetts. The campus is nice, quiet."

"So what, you're in the ninth grade?" Jaleesa asked.

"No, I'm going to the eleventh in September."

"Oh, wow, I'm going to the eighth grade. But I swear I can't wait to get out of school and be on my own. My dad's driving me crazy."

"Does he really know Diddy?"

"Believe it or not, yeah, from back in the day when he played football," she said.

"So, what about your mom?" Tamika asked curiously. "Is she here?"

"My mom's a nurse. She had to work, so I got stuck hanging out with my dad all day. Boring."

"Are they still married?"

"No, they never got married."

"What kind of work does your dad do?" Tamika asked, wondering what Keith did for a living.

"Real estate. My grandfather had the biggest agency in the area and then my dad took it over after he died. I work there during the day sometimes."

"So, what do you do there?" Tamika asked.

"I just do some computer stuff. Get information, type in things, stuff like that."

Tamika nodded.

"It's a summer job, no big deal. It's not like I get paid or anything. He just does it to keep me out of trouble. I accidently broke his car window a few weeks ago, so I'm supposed to be paying for it through slave labor. So, you been around yet?"

"Around where, town?"

"Yeah."

"No, not yet. How is it?"

"Pitiful."

Tamika's cell rang and she looked at the number, thankful for the interruption. "I gotta get this, okay?"

Jaleesa nodded. "A'ight, check you later." She walked away just as Tamika's cell rang a second time.

"Hey, Dad," Tamika said eagerly. "How are you?"

"Hey, babe. I'm fine. Happy Fourth of July. How are you?"

"Fine," Tamika said as the music changed and an upbeat song played.

"Sounds like you found yourself a party to go to."

"Not mine. It's Mom's party or rather her friend's party."

"Grace Hunter?"

"Yeah."

Malcolm laughed. "She's still around, huh?"

"Apparently. Anyway, she's having another birthday party. She had three already since we've been down here."

"I believe it, knowing Grace. Is your mom around? Her cell is off again. She's gotta find a new battery for that phone of hers."

"She's around someplace," Tamika said, then looked around until she spotted her still dancing. "Can she call you back? She's doing the electric slide right now."

"The electric slide? Wow, that's an old one. I'm surprised she remembers how to do it."

Tamika watched her mother and chuckled. "Actually she looks pretty good out there."

"So, what do you think about Fraser so far?"

"I haven't really seen it yet. It's hot, I know that."

"Yeah, Georgia definitely gets hot this time of year. So, how's the cleaning out going?" Malcolm asked.

"Wait, here comes Mom now," Tamika said as Laura walked over laughing with Keith right beside her. Tamika held her cell phone up. "It's Dad, he wants to talk to you."

Laura took the phone as Keith discreetly made himself scarce. "Hello," she began.

"The electric slide?" Malcolm asked.

"Yeah, how about it? I can't believe I still know how," she said, laughing. They talked for a few more minutes and then she gave the phone back to Tamika and walked away.

Her mood had suddenly taken a sharp decline.

She walked through the revelry to Grace's house and slipped in the kitchen door. Not expecting to see anyone there, she was surprised to see Grace standing at the kitchen counter with a huge fruit bowl on one side and a sheet cake on the other side. Grace looked up, hearing her enter. "Hey, lady of leisure, how's it going? You having a good time out there?" Grace asked while cutting a cake into equal-size miniature squares.

Laura smiled. "Having a blast. This is exactly what I needed. I haven't danced so much in years. I'm seriously ready to just have some fun. I'm tired of rules and being responsible. It's time to just let loose."

"I hear you, girl. Just don't let loose too much."

"Me? Nah, I know exactly what I'm doing." They cracked up laughing.

At that moment Keith walked in. "Hello, ladies. Grace, you need any help carrying something out?"

"Sure," she said, pointing at two plates of cake already cut into servable sizes. He picked up the plates, then spared a moment to smile at Laura.

When he walked out, Laura looked at Grace. Grace just shook her head. "Girl, like I said before, if I didn't know any better I'd say that man has the hots for you, big-time."

"And like I said before, it's a good thing you know better, isn't it? I already have a man who's driving me crazy with his drama." She sat down at the counter. "I don't know, Grace, I guess he's just bored with me. Hell, I'm bored with me."

Grace sat down across from her. "So spice things up a bit, get your groove on—within reason, that is."

"Yeah, easy for you to say."

"And just as easy for you to do."

"Don't mind me. I'm just moaning. I'm fine really."

"Oh yeah? I don't know about that, 'cause a few minutes ago you looked like you'd lost your best friend."

"Actually, I think I just found her again." They held hands across the counter.

"Come on, enough of this sappy stuff. Let's go have us some fun." They stood, hugged, then went back outside.

"Hey," Keith said, obviously waiting for Laura.

"Hey yourself."

"So, can we get together and talk? Seems every time I come near, you run away."

"I do not," she said slyly.

"Yeah, you do. It's like you're afraid of me."

"I'm not afraid of you, Keith."

"So let's go someplace and talk. I'd like to catch up. See what you've been doing all this time."

"What about your daughter's mother? Isn't she here tonight?"

"Actually we don't exactly travel in the same circles."

"Oh, I see. Sounds familiar."

"But, as a matter of fact, she is here tonight, to pick up Jaleesa, so…" he said, then licked his lips and she knew right then that Grace was right. There was an attraction, and to her surprise, at this moment it felt as though it was very much mutual. "So, I'm free and at your disposal."

"Really? Okay, I guess we can do that talk thing, then," she said, then glanced around the immediate area, seeing two seats on the deck. "How about over there?"

He looked around, seeing too many people around them.

"Actually, I was thinking that we might need a bit more privacy. You know, for what I'd like to say," he said, moving in closer to whisper into her ear. "We could go someplace."

"Mom, can we go now? I'm tired," Tamika said, walking up to her.

"Sure, honey," Laura said, looking at Keith regretfully.

"I have an idea. Since Jaleesa's mother is taking her home, I can have her drop Tamika off too."

"Or I can take the car and you can get a ride home from your friend."

Laura looked at Tamika, then at Keith. "You two are extremely helpful but I think I'd better drive Tamika home myself. Thanks anyway, Keith."

"Mom, come on, this isn't my first rodeo. You're having fun, so stay. I'll be fine driving back. It's right around the corner. Really, I'll go straight there and I'll be there in a few minutes, promise."

"I don't know," Laura said.

"I can't stop anyplace 'cause I don't know anybody down here. It's still mostly daylight and I'll call you as soon as I get there."

Laura looked at her, considering the suggestion. It wasn't as though Tamika couldn't drive. At sixteen and a half she had her license and she was a very experienced driver. So there'd be no real harm in letting her take the car a few blocks. "Fine, all right, okay," she said. "Here're the keys. Be careful, drive slowly, and call me as soon as you get there. No playing on the road and stay off the cell phone, got it?"

Tamika nodded excitedly, trying to hold back her eager anticipation. Laura reluctantly handed over the keys and watched Tamika drive off slowly and carefully.

"She'll be fine," Keith said as he rested his hands on her shoulders. "Come on, let's dance."

chapter 15

Tamika

The idea of spending another minute at the old folks' party was just not going to happen. Watching them dance to the oldies, laughing and talking about the "good old days" while listening to music sung and performed by grandparents was scary. And expecting her to enjoy the whole thing was insane. But she had to admit they were funny, at least for a while. But seriously, she had to get out of there. Enough was definitely enough.

Tamika leaned back and relaxed, enjoying the peace and serenity of the short drive. It was only a few blocks but it was something. And it said a lot that her mother gave her the keys and trusted her at least for a while. The top was down, the breeze was blowing and her music played on the speakers. Now, this was freedom. She still couldn't believe that her mother allowed her to take the car back to the house.

She wasn't sure if it had something to do with Jaleesa's dad or hanging with the oldies, but either way she was thrilled not to still be there.

After about ten minutes on the road the freedom she enjoyed had come to an end as she pulled up in front of the house and parked behind the other small car. She called her mother and told her that she arrived safely. As soon as she got out of the car and started walking to the front porch, she noticed that the porch light had been turned off. There was also a light on in the living room window and the front door was open. There was someone in the house. Her heart started beating fast. She stepped up on the porch to see a figure out of the corner of her eye.

"Hello?"

"Laura, is that you?" a woman's voice asked.

"No," Tamika said, moving closer.

"Tamika, baby, is that you? It's your aunt Syl."

"Aunt Sylvia," Tamika repeated.

"Of course, who else were you expecting? The porch light blew out."

She looked up at the light, then walked over and saw her aunt Sylvia sitting in one of the rocking chairs on the front porch with a glass of water in one hand and a fan in the other. "Hi, Aunt Syl. Mom didn't tell me that you were coming back tonight."

"Honey child, I forgot how hot this place is. Thank God for central air-conditioning. I don't know how your grandmother and grandfather dealt with it all those years. Hell, I don't know how I dealt with it for the last two years. I must have been outta my mind."

"Yeah, I know, it is definitely hot."

"But it's hotter inside than it is out here. At least there's a breeze every once in a while." She fanned herself as she took a sip of water.

"How's your sick friend doing?" Tamika asked.

"My sick friend?"

"Yeah, Mom told me that you went to visit a friend."

Sylvia chuckled. "Honey child, my friend is six foot two and is as healthy as a horse, or should I say stud? You know that's where I'm moving, don't you?"

"You're moving in with a man?" Tamika asked.

"Yes, and why not?"

"Aunt Sylvia!" Tamika said, shocked.

"What? Uh-huh, thought your old auntie was past it, didn't you? That'll teach you."

Tamika looked away. "Actually, I try not to think about things like that. Eww."

"Really? I thought your mother mentioned that you had a boyfriend, some rapper person."

"I did, kinda."

"Kinda? What does that mean? Either you have a boyfriend or you don't. If you do, then you'd better be cautious and start thinking about it."

"Justin, that's his name. He and I broke up, more or less."

She laughed. "You young people are a trip. In my day there was no question about a breakup, none of that half-stepping."

"Okay, Justin and I just left it hangin' before I left. I haven't called and neither has he. But I'm kinda talking to this guy named Sean now."

"Sean. I knew a Sean once," she interrupted, smiling happily.

Tamika smiled too. "Anyway, since it doesn't look like I'm gonna be heading back home anytime soon, Sean might be coming down here. His grandparents live near here."

"And you like this Sean?"

Tamika nodded. "Yeah."

"An actual straight answer. Impressive."

"So, Aunt Syl, when did you get in?" Tamika asked, awkwardly changing the subject.

"A couple of hours ago. I told your mother that I'd be stopping by this evening. I need to finish packing up the rest of my things tomorrow morning."

"I guess she forgot."

"I don't see how. I reminded her yesterday when I called her. Huh, and they say us old people can't remember anything. Where is she?" she asked, looking behind Tamika.

"She's still at a party over at her friend's house."

"What friend?"

"Ms. Hunter."

"Grace Hunter?"

Tamika nodded.

Sylvia started laughing. "Oh Lordy, that's trouble all over the place. How was the party?"

"Wacked."

She chuckled. "So I guess you left early."

"Uh-huh," Tamika said.

"Not particularly your style, huh?"

"No, definitely not," she said, then paused. "It was a'ight, I guess, if you like that kind of thing. It just wasn't me. I wasn't feeling it. When I left they were tearing the roof off the sucker with a flashlight."

Sylvia started laughing. "Ah yes, the Funkadelics."

"The what?" she asked.

"The Funkadelics. I don't think you're ready for them just yet."

"So you know who they are, huh?"

"Oh yeah. Many a night I tore a few roofs off the mother myself."

"What?"

Sylvia chuckled. "Never mind, you had to be there. You see, I wasn't always in my seventies, you know, honey child."

"Anyway, Mom gave me the car keys so I left."

"I get the picture," Sylvia said, smiling and chuckling. "Was your mom having a good time?"

"Yeah, she was tripping, dancing and joking around. I think there were more of her old friends there too."

"Well, she's allowed."

"So, why did you say that's trouble all over the place?" Tamika asked.

"Still waters run deep."

"Huh? I don't get it."

"You gotta understand, your mother was just as sweet and quiet as you please growing up. She was a good girl, didn't get into any trouble, even helped her parents like she should. Listened and obeyed and did exactly what was expected of her, for the most part anyway. But when she came home from college that first year it was like she was a different person. Together with Grace they caused some kind of trouble that one summer. They were hell on wheels."

"Mom? My mom?" Tamika said, finding it hard to believe.

"She wasn't always your mom. Now, Grace is bad enough by herself already, but you put those two together and you're just asking for it."

Tamika couldn't believe what she was hearing. At first she thought that her great-aunt was just exaggerating or just talking. She was known to do that.

"So, what happened after that?"

"Nothing. She sowed her wild oats and that's it. She went right back to her old self. That's when she met your father. She settled right down, never heard a peep from her since."

"Until now," Tamika said.

"Well, that remains to be seen."

"So, what exactly did she do?" Tamika asked.

"For that you need to ask her."

"She's not gonna tell me."

"She might. I don't see why not."

"She won't, no way. We don't talk."

"What do you mean you don't talk?"

"We don't talk." Tamika still didn't clarify.

"Well, that doesn't make any sense. Of course you talk. You have to talk."

"Well, we talk. I mean, I talk but she doesn't listen."

"So you talk and she doesn't listen and I bet if I ask her, then she'd tell me that she talks and you don't listen to her."

"I listen," Tamika protested.

"That's what you say. What does she say? Sounds like a lot of she said, she said to me."

"Huh?"

Sylvia chuckled. "Never mind, this ought to be an interesting summer."

Tamika didn't get it so she chalked the whole thing up to her aunt's momentary delusional insanity. Just then the sky exploded. They both looked up as firecrackers lit up the surrounding area. Then, like a chain reaction, they saw fireworks in another direction. The display lasting for twenty minutes, they sat out enjoying the spectacular splendor in the sky.

"Bet you haven't seen anything like that."

"We used to go to the fireworks in the city."

"You used to? Why'd you stop?"

"I usually hang with my friends," Tamika said, seeing the irony. She'd hang out with her friends while her mother stayed home, and tonight it was the exact opposite. "So, you staying over tonight, right?"

"Might as well. Don't look like I'm gonna be doing any packing this late," she said, then stood up and stretched. "All right, I gonna get me upstairs. The bedroom air conditioner must have cooled the room by now. Are you coming in now?" she asked as she stopped and turned.

"In a little bit," Tamika said, deciding to sit out and enjoy the breeze starting to blow.

"All right. Don't stay out too late, there's a storm coming."

"Okay." Tamika stayed out sitting on the porch rail.

She was thinking about her mother and what she had done that summer. Whatever it was it must have been something. She smiled at the possibility, hoping that one day she'd find out.

A half hour later, still not tired, she went in and sat at the table checking her digital photos. Some were really pretty good. Afterward she went online to see the particulars of the *National Geographic*'s amateur photo submission requirements. They didn't seem too difficult, but they asked for professional-quality work, something she wasn't sure she could pull off. She continued on other sites, surfing in general.

Curiously she typed in Fraser, and was surprised that a town so small actually had a Web site. She read the town's history, schedule of events and even about the big Independence Day fair and celebration. The history was just as her mother told her from way back with her ancestor General Joseph Fraser and his family. She couldn't believe it. Suddenly she felt kind of proud to be connected. Having a whole town named after you was definitely impressive.

There was a map showing the main street, schools and stores and, of course, the town hall. She started going through the local people with the help of her mother's year-books. She looked up Grace Hunter and found out that she worked for the local newspaper that her father, the mayor, owned. Then, not surprisingly, Keith Tyler had been a local hero. He was a professional football player but had resigned because of medical and personal problems.

A half hour later she decided to quit when she heard the rumble of thunder in the distance moving closer. Her aunt Sylvia was right, there was a storm coming, and the last thing she needed was for her laptop, her only link to the civilized world, to get fried from a lightning strike or a power surge.

It was way after midnight and her mother still wasn't home. It started to rain as soon as she climbed into bed. A few minutes later, lulled by the storm, she fell asleep. Then, just after two in the morning, she was awakened by a noise. She listened in the darkness, not hearing anything except the distant thunder. But that wasn't the noise that woke her up. It was laughter, her mother's laughter, and it was coming from outside.

She went downstairs and peeked out the front window. Her mom was on the porch talking to someone. A few seconds later she realized that she was talking to Keith Tyler. She listened.

They talked about high school and how he never really talked to her and how he was popular and she was the quiet, studious one. They mentioned other people they went to school with in a kind of "where are they now?" thing. Then she talked about her old job and he talked about his short-lived career as a professional football player and how he'd gotten hurt and had to leave the game. He started telling her how much he regretted not knowing her in high school and how they might have been really close.

Tamika watched as he moved closer, then reached up and

touched her mother's face. He leaned in slowly. Without thinking, Tamika opened the front door wide and fast, startling them apart. "Mom, is that you? The porch light blew out."

"Yes, it's me," Laura said.

"Hey, I thought that was you," Tamika said.

"Hey, sweetie. What are you still doing up? It's late. Is everything okay?"

"Yeah, I just couldn't sleep and I heard a noise out here, so I came down to check it out." She glanced at Keith hard.

"It was probably the storm coming back."

"Listen, Laura, we'll continue this later," Keith said, then took Laura's hand and kissed it. "Good night."

Tamika frowned, grossed out by the old-time wannabe player trying to hit on her mom. She watched as he walked back to his car, got in, waved, then drove off. Her mom stayed on the porch smiling and waving.

"Aunt Sylvia's here," Tamika said as her mother headed to the front door.

She stopped. "Here, already? I thought she was visiting a friend for a few days."

"She's back," Tamika said. "She's upstairs asleep. I didn't know she had a boyfriend."

Laura smiled, shaking her head. "There's a lot about your aunt that you don't know."

"I'm beginning to see that," Tamika said. Laura turned back to the front door. "What are you wearing? That's not what you had on when I left you at the party."

Laura looked down and chuckled. "Oh yeah, we were out dancing and there was a sudden downpour. My clothes got soaked so I borrowed something from Grace."

"The top is too tight, your stomach's out and the skirt is way too short," Tamika said of the well-fitted midriff top and outrageous skirt.

Laura chuckled again. "I just borrowed it. It's not like I'm gonna wear it all the time. But for your information, I got a lot of compliments on this outfit."

"From Keith Tyler, no doubt," Tamika surmised.

"Yes, as a matter of fact he liked me in it."

"I'd bet he'd like you out of it more."

"Excuse me?" Laura said.

"I thought Ms. Hunter was gonna drive you home."

"It was late and after dancing all night Grace was tired, so Keith was kind enough to drop me off on his way home."

"So, exactly what's up with him?" Tamika asked.

"What do you mean?"

"I mean, can't he see that big old wedding band and rock on your finger?"

"Tamika, Keith knows I'm a married woman. He's just being nice, that's all."

"It doesn't look like that's all to me."

"We're old friends, we go back," Laura said.

"Isn't he the one who rubber-stamped the same thing in everybody's yearbook?"

"Yes," she said, smiling.

"And that's okay now?" Tamika asked.

"That was a long time ago. We were kids."

"So now that you're adults it's okay."

"Let's just say that after a while time passes and you learn to let bygones be bygones."

"I don't like him and I don't trust him," Tamika said as a burst of lightning flashed across the sky.

"You don't know him."

"You don't know Justin but you don't like him."

"I never said that I didn't like Justin. I said that you didn't need to get tied down to one boy just yet. I don't know why you twist things around. I say one thing and you hear something completely opposite. Besides, this is totally different," Laura said. Tamika didn't reply. "Okay, so you don't like him. Tell me why."

"I don't know, there's just something about him."

"Well, I guess that it's a good thing that he's not your friend, then, isn't it?" Laura said.

"Fine, whatever. I'm just saying." Thunder rolled, sounding closer.

"Tamika, we're just friends. You have nothing to worry about. Nothing's gonna happen between us. I'm still married to your father, okay? Okay?"

"Yeah, okay," Tamika said reluctantly as lightning flashed and thunder rumbled at nearly the same time.

"Now, come on in. It's late and it looks like that storm is coming back this way."

They walked inside and Laura locked the front door.

"Okay, I'll see you tomorrow morning," she said, continuing upstairs. Then she stopped when Tamika didn't follow. "You're not coming upstairs to bed?"

"Yeah, in a minute. I'm gonna get a glass of water first."

"All right, don't stay up too late. Good night."

"Night," Tamika said, still annoyed by her mother's blind devotion. She went into the kitchen, poured herself a glass of cold water and decided that she was going to find out exactly what Keith Tyler wanted. The more she thought about it, the more skeptical she got. Keith reminded her of Justin, and that was definitely something to be concerned about.

She knew his type. Justin was his type and her mother had

no idea what she was doing. She couldn't see him for what he was. Completely battery-charged, she unplugged the laptop from the wall socket and went online. She was online when her cell rang. It was late, way after midnight, but she still answered. "Hello."

"Hi. I hope it's okay that I called this late. I wanted to catch up with you. Are you busy?" Sean said.

"I can't talk right now, Sean," she said as she continued surfing, looking for more information on Keith Tyler. Being that he was a professional football player and apparent PR whore, there were hundreds of sites listed for him.

"Okay, it's just that I saw that you were online so I just wanted to call and say sorry that I missed you tonight."

"Missed me, what? Look, Sean, you don't even really know me. Anyway, I can't deal with that right now. My mom has gone crazy. It's like she's trying to be a teenager all over again. As soon as we got here she changed, hanging out with her friends all the time."

"So what's wrong with that?" he asked.

"You're kidding me, right? How would you like it if it was your mom?"

"No big deal. So, what, she's having fun, right?"

"She's a mom—my mom. She can't be doing that."

"Doing what? Having fun?" he asked.

"Yeah," she said, then realized how silly she sounded. "Never mind, you don't get it. She's old, she needs to just clean out this house and that's it. I want to go home. This place is tired and old and pathetic."

"Is Fraser really that bad?" he asked solemnly.

"Yes. I hate it here. The people are all stupid and country. It's like being stuck in the Dark Ages. I hate everything about this place."

"I'm sorry to hear that."

"Whatever."

"You know what? You're a lot different than before."

"What do you mean?"

"I mean I don't get why you're so stressed over this. You need to chill. If your mom wants to have a little fun, then what's the big deal? She's allowed."

"Oh, please, you don't even know. The big deal is that she needs to chill so I can go back home. I have things to do."

"Justin, right?"

"No."

"Look, I don't know your family, I'm just saying—"

"That's right, you don't know my family. You don't know anything about my family or me. So don't be getting all up in my business, trying to analyze me."

"You're right. I guess I'll talk to you whenever."

"Yeah, right, whatever," she said.

"You know what? You're really different. I guess you and Justin deserve each other after all. Later." He hung up.

She had just dumped everything on Sean and now she felt horrible.

chapter 16

Laura

Laura danced upstairs, down the hall, into the bedroom and bathroom and as she put on her pajamas. The good feeling had surrounded her and she was loving it. The music still plugged in her head played on and on. She'd forgotten how much fun she could have just hanging out.

She climbed into bed, but the music and happiness wouldn't let her sleep. She lay back thinking about the party. What had started out as an outdoor picnic soon moved inside. The rain poured outside and they danced, laughed and joked inside. She had too much fun and, of course, hanging with Keith didn't hurt.

All of four years she'd had a crush on him while they were in high school. And all of four years he completely ignored her. But tonight she was the only person he saw and it felt great having a man's full attention.

Just as her thoughts focused on that, a quick sudden pang of guilt hit her. Malcolm. She wasn't exactly being unfaithful, but she couldn't actually say that she hadn't been flirting either.

As soon as she half dozed off her cell rang. "Hello."

"I got your number from Grace. Hope you don't mind."

"Keith?"

"Yeah, is this a bad time?"

"No, not at all. How are you?"

"You mean since the last time you saw me about an hour ago?" he said. She giggled. "I'm okay, you?"

"I am fantastic." She breathed out slowly.

"I'd have to agree with that. You are kinda fantastic."

"Yeah, right."

"No, really. I guess I never took the time to really hang out with you, but I gotta say that I really enjoyed myself with you this evening. You are one beautiful woman—mind, body and spirit."

"You think so, huh?" Her body began tingling nicely.

"I know so," he moaned into the receiver. She didn't say anything. "Are you still there?"

"Yes," she whispered.

"Did I embarrass you?"

"No," she said, smiling, trying to remember the last time her husband had even glanced at her appreciatively. After he'd had the affair with his coworker last year, she went on a serious diet and hit the gym as if it were the only place on earth. She'd lost weight, gotten into shape and started wearing stylish clothes and he never said a word.

"Sorry," he apologized anyway. "It's just that I can't remember having as good a time with anyone in a long, long time. Just standing out on the front porch talking to you was nice."

"Yeah, it was kinda nice."

"So..." he began, then paused a few seconds. "May I see you again?"

"I'm not sure my husband would appreciate me hanging out with a single man."

"I understand. If I had you as my woman I know I'd have a problem with that too. He's a very lucky man." She didn't respond. "So I'd better say good-night, before I really give him something to worry about. Good night, Laura."

"Good night, Keith."

She closed her cell and lay back slowly. So that's what it felt like to have Keith Tyler call you in the middle of the night. She smiled, then giggled until she fell asleep.

The next morning she got up late and, to her surprise, Tamika was already up and in the kitchen. She was making pancakes and talking to Sylvia, who was sitting at the kitchen table drinking something hot from a mug.

"Morning," Laura said, yawning and covering her mouth.

"Well, good morning, sleepyhead," Sylvia said.

"Morning, Mom. How many pancakes do you want?"

"Pancakes? You don't cook pancakes."

"Aunt Sylvia just showed me. It's easy, watch." She shuffled a spatula under and flipped a pancake over, nearly missing the side of the pan. "See, easy."

"Not bad. Good for you. But I'm gonna pass on breakfast. I think I ate too much last night." She walked over and picked up the teakettle on the stove, still heavy with hot water. She grabbed a mug and found a tea bag, then began dunking it slowly as she sat down next to Sylvia.

"Sure it wasn't something you drank?"

"No, Aunt Sylvia. And besides, Grace is in AA. She didn't have any alcohol there last night, just soda and punch." She sipped the hot drink and grimaced. It was hot and strong and exactly what she needed.

"Uh-huh, like nobody else can bring booze to a party and spike a punch bowl."

"I wasn't drinking last night. I just danced too much and had too much fun."

"Well, there's nothing wrong with that."

Tamika placed a stack of pancakes on the table and sat down. She grabbed a few, added syrup, then dug in as if she hadn't eaten in days.

Sylvia grabbed a couple of pancakes, added a ton of butter and half a bottle of syrup, then cut into them with a knife and fork. Laura just sipped her tea.

"So, what do we have to do today?" Tamika asked.

Laura sighed. "We're gonna help Aunt Syl with the last of her things, then start sorting things out, what we're gonna keep or toss out. Also the Realtor specialist I spoke to in Boston might be coming by this morning. She's supposed to call if she can make it today."

"What's a Realtor specialist? Like an agent?" Sylvia asked.

"No, they don't actually sell the house but they give you ideas on how to make the house more sellable. They talk to you about improvements, remodeling, staging and things like that. Since we're selling it ourselves I hired her to give us some advice."

"Oh, heavens," Sylvia muttered, disheartened.

"What?" Laura asked, seeing her saddened expression.

Sylvia shook her head slowly. "Nothing, nothing. It's just that this house has been in your family for so long, it'll be a shame to just let it go just like that. Thank goodness your dear mother isn't alive to see this. It would break her heart."

"I don't have a choice, Aunt Syl. The upkeep on this place is too expensive now that I'm not working and it's too far away for me to keep an eye on it. I spoke to the Realtor specialist and she seemed to think that we could sell it without too much trouble. I know it's been in the family forever, but I don't see any other alternative. I don't want to rent it out furnished. I'd rather sell it than to have someone trash or destroy it. We just have to get the place together so she can check it out. I'm sure she's gonna have some things to suggest we do."

"What kind of things?" Tamika asked.

"Oh, just ways to help make the house move quickly—presentation, curb appeal, things like that," she said. The room got quiet after that. Laura could feel the tension in the air. It was obvious she wasn't the only one regretting her decision.

After breakfast the three of them gathered boxes and started packing up the remainder of Sylvia's things. By the time they finished it was after twelve o'clock. And there were over fifteen boxes lined up by the front door.

"Honey child, I don't know where I got all that stuff and I have no idea where I'm gonna put it all. Roberta's gonna have a fit when she sees me bringing all this with me."

"Roberta's coming?" Laura asked.

"That's what I told you the other day when I called, remember?"

"I meant to call you back. We had a bad connection and I couldn't really hear you." Laura exaggerated since there was static on the line and she was too busy looking at Keith.

"Don't matter about that. She'll be here in a few minutes to pick me up anyway."

"She's picking you up? What about your car outside?" Tamika asked, assuming it was hers.

"My car?" Sylvia asked, then looked at Laura. "Oh, you mean the car parked out front. I wouldn't worry about that right now, although the keys are in the counter drawer just in case you need to move it."

"I still have the rental. We're fine," Laura said.

"Well then, maybe Tamika would like to use it."

Laura looked at Sylvia, then to Tamika. "We'll see."

An hour later Roberta, Sylvia's daughter, arrived.

"All this stuff goes?" Roberta asked. Sylvia nodded. "Mom, where are we gonna put everything? The apartment is already busting at the seams, and if you store one more thing in my house my husband is gonna divorce me."

"Of course he won't, and if he does, then good riddance," Sylvia said.

Tamika chuckled, Laura shook her head and Roberta was just plain exasperated as Sylvia laughed.

The four loaded all the boxes into Roberta's minivan, then said their goodbyes. Roberta got into the driver's seat and Sylvia walked back to the house. Laura met her on the front steps. "Are you sure you know what you're doing?"

"Truthfully, I don't have a clue."

"And Malcolm, what's this thing with him?"

"Same answer."

"Honey child, somebody needs to call that man on the other side of the world and clue him in. He's losing and he doesn't even know it. There's no sense half-stepping like this. I told Tamika the same thing."

"I know we'll get it together one of these days."

"Not if he's halfway 'round the other side of the planet. You need face-to-face."

"Goodbye, Aunt Sylvia," Laura said, hugging her and dismissing the conversation. Sylvia nodded, then waved as she got into the packed car and they drove off.

"Are they gonna be all right?" Tamika asked, hearing them battling about something as they drove away.

"Sure, Aunt Syl and Roberta are like that. They complain

and battle like crazy, but just try to come between them. They'll be fine."

They stayed out on the porch for a while talking. "We got a lot done today," Laura said.

Tamika nodded. "What exactly are we going to do with all that other stuff?"

"Sell it mostly, I guess. Maybe have a huge estate sale or yard sale."

"Not everything, though, right?"

"No, not everything."

"I found some letters and a ledger in the attic the other day."

"The slave ledger?"

"Yeah, you knew about it?"

"Oh yeah, it's been in this family for a long, long time. I remember my mother showing me it years ago."

"Don't you think we should do something with it? I mean, we can't just put it out with the trash or anything. It's history—our history."

Laura smiled. A glimmer of appreciation had finally emerged from her daughter. "No, of course not. So what do you suggest?"

"I don't know. Maybe we can have it appraised first."

"Good idea. Let's do that."

"Cool," Tamika said readily. "I was online the other day and I found a couple of antique shops and a historical society near Fraser. Maybe we can contact them."

"Good idea. Why don't you give them a call?"

Tamika nodded. "So what now."

"Well, it's still early," Laura said, glancing at her watch. "The real estate specialist hasn't called, so I don't think she'll be coming by today. We have a ton more boxes and things to go through, so I guess we could start going through and clearing out the other rooms or attic or basement or maybe take a break."

"Let's take a break," Tamika quickly suggested. "After boxing up the rest of Aunt Sylvia's things and her walking down memory lane every two minutes or every time she picked something up, I seriously need to chill."

"Okay, you take a break. I'm gonna go for a quick run. Want to join me?" Laura asked, remembering a time when she and Tamika jogged together.

"Nah, maybe next time."

"Okay," Laura said, then went upstairs to change her clothes. A few minutes later she was out the door running down the street.

It felt good. She passed places she hadn't seen in years. Some were gone, some hadn't changed a bit. She waved at people and even stopped to chat with a friend of her mother's who lived around the corner. By the time she turned and headed back she was sweating, breathless and exhausted, but it felt good.

She hadn't run in a few days and her body obviously missed the strenuous routine she'd undertaken for the past six months. She stopped at the front yard, stretched out her legs, thighs and arms, then slowly went into the house. Tamika, bless her heart, had a large bottle of cold water wrapped in a dish towel waiting for her on the step.

"I'm back," she hollered.

"Dad called. He wants you to call him back."

Laura took several swigs of water, then went upstairs as she auto-dialed her husband. He didn't pick up so she left a message, then took a quick shower.

When she stepped out of the bathroom wrapped in a towel, Tamika met her in the hall. "Mom, your cell was ringing a minute ago."

"Okay," she said, presuming it was Malcolm returning her call. She started getting dressed in shorts and a T-shirt. Her cell rang and a few minutes later she was changed into a low-cut summer sundress and coming downstairs looking like a Hollywood movie star with dark sunglasses and a wide-brimmed straw hat. She was checking her scant makeup in the foyer mirror when Tamika walked up.

"Mom, check you out, where're you going?"

"Out."

"Out where?"

"Out to late lunch with a friend."

"What friend? Grace Hunter or Keith Tyler?" The last name was said with definite attitude.

"A friend, Tamika," Laura said, then saw Tamika's face instantly change. Her disapproval was obvious. "I'll be back in a while."

"Are you okay? I mean with Dad having to stay longer."

"He has to stay longer?" Laura asked. "I called him back earlier but couldn't get through."

Tamika nodded. "He called my cell when he couldn't get through to you. Are you okay about it?"

"I don't have a choice, do I? I'll be back later."

"So, what about the real estate person maybe coming over later?"

"I doubt she's still coming, but if she does you can do that," Laura said as she grabbed the keys and headed to the front door.

"Mom," Tamika called out. Laura turned. Tamika opened her mouth but decided it was no use even getting into it. "Never mind. I guess I'll take care of it."

"Thanks, be back soon."

"So, what am I supposed to do after that?"

Laura shrugged. "I don't know, check out Fraser. There's a bicycle in the garage out back. See you later."

Angry was an understatement.

A quick twenty-minute drive and Laura was sitting in a small local restaurant drinking iced tea and waiting for her chicken-salad sandwich to arrive. Seeing her friend had made all her drama null and void.

Now wearing studious eyeglasses and dressed in a very professional business suit, Grace yawned wearily. "I'm beat," she said, then sipped her sweetened iced tea and cupped her head in the palm of her hand and elbowed the table.

"It was a great party. Thanks again for inviting us."

"My pleasure. I hope Tamika wasn't too bored by all us old heads out there dancing and clowning around."

"She was fine."

"Good. So what's up with you and Keith? He like jumped out of his skin when I said I was gonna take you home. The last time I saw that man move that fast he was on the football field."

Laura chuckled, flattered by the comparison. "He's just being friendly."

"I don't know about that. I hope you know what you're doing with him."

"I'm not doing anything, we're just friends. He's harmless."

"Yeah, right. I heard that before."

"Don't worry, just friends," Laura said. "Okay, what's this emergency lunch that was so important?"

Grace smiled. "I have a proposition for you."

"What kind of proposition?"

"You know I still work at the newspaper, right?" she began. Laura nodded. "Well, I also freelance for this other magazine from time to time. Anyway, I was telling my magazine editor that I have a friend in town who is a brilliant writer and then I mentioned that you should write something for them like a freelance article. She was very interested."

"You did what?" Laura said.

"I told her that you were the editor of your college newspaper and that you were taking a break from writing an unbelievable women's lit novel."

"You did what?" she repeated.

"Okay, so maybe I exaggerated slightly."

"Slightly? Sounds like you all but handed her my Pulitzer prize acceptance speech."

"Now who's exaggerating?"

"Tell me you didn't."

"Oh, please, don't be so affronted. It's a great idea. You're not working right now and the magazine will pay you some pretty nice pocket change."

"No, absolutely not," Laura said.

"Why not?" Grace asked.

"Because."

"Because why?" Grace persisted.

"Because," Laura insisted.

"Because? What kind of argument is that?"

"Just because I say so."

Grace smirked. "I'm a mom too, remember? That doesn't work on me."

"Because," Laura said, getting more and more agitated. "Because, oh, I don't know. Because I just can't. I haven't actually written anything serious in years."

"But you wrote for your advertising agency, right? And you always wanted to write a bestseller, right? Well, this is the perfect time to get started. Writing a small piece for the magazine would be perfect."

"Grace, that was a long, long time ago. The last thing I actually wrote was an employee evaluation. When I left I was the managing advertising director. I oversaw ad campaigns and made presentations. That's radio and television commercials, not full-length, in-depth magazine articles. What would I even write about?"

"I don't know, something. Coming back home after so long, the changes you see in the place, your parents' house, you and your daughter. I don't know."

Laura shook her head slightly, yet considered the idea as Grace looked on. "Come on, it'll be fun. We'll work together just like we said we would all those years ago."

"Okay, okay, I'll tell you what. I'll think about it."

"Seriously think about it?" Grace offered.

"Yes, seriously think about it," Laura promised.

"Fair enough. I'll be out of town on assignment over the next week and a half. You have until then. But you better say yes or else," Grace said happily and smiled.

Laura smiled too, and then instantly they both broke out laughing. When the laughter subsided Grace started rubbing her temples again as she yawned.

"Ugh, whose idea was it to keep Independence Day on a weekday? And what was I thinking, partying all night long on a weeknight? I used to be able to do it with no problem. I swear I must be getting old. I have absolutely no stamina anymore."

Laura smiled and shook her head. "Girl, we're all getting old."

"You're not supposed to say that. You're supposed to say that our inner youth will never get old or something like that."

"Yeah, okay, you keep on believing that."

"What, you think we're getting old?"

"I know we are. There's no way we can do now what we did then," Laura admitted.

"Sure we can." Grace smiled. They laughed again. "So, speaking of youth, what's Tamika up to?"

"Chillin'."

"She's a sweet girl. You're so lucky. You have the perfect family."

"Where did you get that idea?"

"You're married with a teenage daughter who's on her way to college. You have it all."

"I have a husband who cheated on me last summer with a coworker who is probably the same coworker he's in Tokyo with right now. Plus I have a daughter I get along with like fire and water. I say one thing, she hears another. It's like we don't speak the same language."

"Men are gonna be men, that's all I have to say about that. Now, as for you and your daughter, you speak the same language. You just forgot how to listen."

"I listen," Laura protested.

"Yeah, you listen like a parent. Try hearing her as a person. You remember what it was like when we were teens. Our parents never listened to us. Loosen up, try walking in her shoes. I think you'll find they fit pretty well. To understand her you need to remember you."

"Me?" Laura asked, not getting it.

"Your mother drove you crazy, Laura. Remember, you complained constantly. We all did. Our parents didn't know a thing back then."

"No, my mom and I got along great. We were best friends."

"Yeah, later after you were grown. But before then, when we were teenagers, you complained all the time that she drove you crazy because she was so overprotective because of Deb."

Laura frowned in denial, and then suddenly she remembered. Laura looked at her friend and smiled. "Oh my God, you're right. I guess I just forgot that part."

"Sure, we have to because that part, the teenage angst, doesn't matter anymore. You became friends and that's all that matters. We had to take one moment at a time to get past all that teenage drama."

Laura nodded. "I guess I need to take a step back and start enjoying the little moments with my teenager. So, since when did you become a shrink?"

"Since I raised two sons," she said jokingly. "Remember, I had my kids a lot earlier than you. I'm through with all that teenage drama."

"Remember all the things we said we'd do?" Laura said.

Grace looked at her strangely. "Like what?"

Laura leaned over and began whispering. "Like we said that we'd go to the high school and get that stupid moose head and rip it down off the wall."

"What moose head?"

"Principal Kilmore's moose head. The one he hung up in the school office. We always said that we'd go back and rip it down one day, remember?"

Grace cracked up. "Girl, I forgot all about that thing. But we can't do it anyway. Kilmore retired and took that stupid thing with him when he left."

"Well, something else, then. Come on, it'll be fun."

"You are crazy, break into the high school and take something. I don't know, but maybe we could—"

"Well, well, well. Hello, ladies." Laura and Grace both looked up, with extremely guilty expressions on their faces. Keith stood at their table, smiling down at them. "This must be my lucky day," he said, looking directly at Laura.

"Hey," Laura said, smiling.

"Keith," Grace said, then sipped her drink.

"I thought I'd grab a quick bite," he said, looking around the crowded restaurant, then at the seat next to Laura. "May I join you?"

"Well..." Laura began.

"Actually, we were just finishing up," Grace said as she tossed her napkin on her empty plate and stood. "I need to get back to work."

"Pity... Are you sure?" he asked as he sat down beside Laura.

"Well, maybe just for a quick refill..." Laura said.

"Help yourself. I've got to get back," Grace said. "Call me later, okay?"

Laura nodded. "Okay, I will. Bye."

The waitress arrived and handed Keith a menu. He looked it over quickly as Laura observed his face.

"You know what, let's get out of here."

"I thought you were hungry."

"I am, but not necessarily for food. Let's go."

"Where?" she asked, not budging.

"There's a nice place I know not too far from here."

"But I've already eaten."

"It's not a restaurant."

"What is it?"

"Trust me," he said easily with that smile.

"Keith, I don't know what kind of game we're playing here, but I think I might be in way over my head. I'm married and I don't cheat on my husband," she said, opening her mouth to say more but deciding against it.

"Why not?" he asked simply.

"Because I don't," she said.

"Interesting."

"What?"

"Well, you didn't say because you were in love with your husband. So how about because you haven't found someone interesting enough to be with, or someone you're comfortable with or maybe someone you're attracted to?"

"I didn't say that."

"But that's what you meant."

She shook her head. "You're putting words in my mouth and I should go."

He smirked slyly and licked his lips. "I could answer that remark in so many different ways," he said, raising his brow provocatively. Laura instantly blushed and looked away, knowing exactly what he was thinking. "I'll tell you what," he began, then reached over and took her hand. "Tomorrow morning I have to go out of town on business for a couple of days. When I get back we'll talk."

"Keith, I'm not who you think I am. I can't—"

"Laura, you're exactly who I think you are and if ever you find yourself...tempted..." He smiled openly, then slid his business card into her hand.

She stared at him, then at the card. Tempted. The word had hung in the air between them like a giant boulder. There was no getting around it. Huge and heavy in meaning, the implication was clear and had far exceeded her stray fantasies.

Tempted. Of course she considered Keith. She'd considered Keith ever since she was in high school. She wondered and fantasized and even wished on occasion, but that was as far as she got. Now the offer had been made. One she'd fantasized about for years.

She slowly slid her hand away from his, nodded, stood, then walked out. She finally caught her breath halfway down the street to the parked car. Tempted.

She looked at the card, then pulled out her cell. "What are you doing this evening?"

chapter 17

Tamika

"**Great,** super, another exciting adventure in Fraser," Tamika muttered to herself as she stepped outside onto the porch and watched her mom drive off. Again. This was getting ridiculous; her mother was hanging out and having more fun than she was.

She tried to call Lisa, but she was at work and couldn't talk. Then she tried to call Sean, but he didn't pick up. And she didn't want to leave a message. After their last conversation she wasn't even sure what to say anyway.

She looked around. Obviously she'd been stuck in the house for too long. Thankfully the weather had cooled down after the storm to somewhere south of hot as hell, but at least it was bearable and she could breathe again. She walked to the sidewalk and looked both ways, trying to decide which way to go. Then she remembered seeing a small strip mall just around the corner and a few blocks away, so she decided to check it out.

She went inside, grabbed her camera and was headed to

the front door just as the doorbell rang. It was the Realtor specialist her mom spoke about. Damn. Of course she'd pick now to show up. Tamika considered not answering, then just telling her to go away and come back later, but she realized that if she wanted to go back to Boston she needed to get all this over with as soon as possible. That meant dealing with this herself.

One extended tour and an hour and a half later the Realtor left. She'd made a list of things to do to quicken the sale. Feeling particularly good having handled everything all by herself, Tamika checked the list, making sure she correctly commented on items that were the most essential. Satisfied that she'd done a fairly complete job, she grabbed her MP3 player and pocketed some cash, then headed outside again.

The bike her mom mentioned was in the garage behind the house. Of course she found more labeled boxes. She pulled it down off the hooks and got on. More used to stationary ellipticals, she easily adjusted.

A few minutes later she paddled up to the small strip mall. She went into store after store and found exactly what she expected: nothing. Slightly disappointed, she noticed a hardware and paint store across the street. Without thinking she hurried over, went in and started looking around. Finding nothing of interest, she did pick up some paint samples as the Realtor specialist suggested and even grabbed a few decorating brochures, mainly for the photographs of course. Just as she walked out of the store and got back on the bike she heard her name called. She turned.

Jaleesa was riding by on her bicycle. "Hey, Tamika, hi," she said excitedly. "I was just asking my dad if he knew where you lived. I wanted to know if you could hang out."

"Hang out?" Tamika asked, looking at her as if she was

nuts. There were no way she would be caught dead hanging out with an eighth-grader. They had absolutely nothing in common. She was a kid. But then again, there was no one else around.

"Yeah, you and me. Want to go into town?"

"I thought this was the town."

"This? Nah, come on, I'll show you."

Tamika looked back at the stores she'd just left. She didn't have much of a choice. "Sure, why not? I just gotta stop at my house first and get my camera."

"Cool." Jaleesa nodded and followed as Tamika led the way back home. They parked their bikes out front. "Is this your house?" she asked.

"It's my mom's house."

"It's big."

"Yeah, it is." Tamika hurried inside, grabbed the ledger with the letters and her camera and placed them in her backpack. When she came back out, Jaleesa was looking up at the house. "I'm ready, let's go," Tamika said.

"Know what? I know this house. My dad has pictures of it in his office. I remember seeing it. I think somebody he knows in this big company he works with sometimes wants to buy it. He sold it to them already."

"Really? This house? My house?"

Jaleesa shrugged. "Yeah, he's got a sold file sticker on it already and everything."

Tamika presumed that she was mistaken. After all, how could he have already sold the house when he didn't even own it?

A few minutes later, the two were enjoying their bike ride and Jaleesa was showing Tamika the sights as they laughed and talked while heading into town.

Tamika noticed that the buildings got progressively larger as they got closer. Gone were the small side streets with quiet neighborhoods. They were replaced with what looked like a tiny city—nothing as large as Boston but still nice. "So, this is Fraser?" Tamika said when they stopped and started walking.

"Fraser, no. This is Elwood. It's right next to Fraser. Fraser is way too small to have any fun. Most of the kids hang here, see?" she said, then waved at a couple of girls about her age crossing the street. Tamika saw that they instantly had an air about themselves. Giggling, they looked at Jaleesa, looked away and just kept walking.

"Were they your friends?" Tamika asked.

"I don't know. Sometimes, I guess."

"They don't seem like it," Tamika added.

"They just act funny sometimes, that's all."

"So, let me guess. They're your friends when they want something or when it comes to copying homework and doing class assignments, right?"

"Sometimes, yeah," Jaleesa said sadly.

"And they don't speak to you?" Tamika asked.

Jaleesa shrugged.

"Jaleesa, you do know that means that they're not really your friends, right?"

"I guess. But I don't have anyone else."

"Sure you do. Who do you talk to when you're in school? Who do you eat lunch with?"

"Nobody."

Tamika suddenly felt bad. She'd always been popular with plenty of friends and never thought about those who ate alone. Besides, she'd always had Lisa. But now Lisa would be leaving. She had other friends but Jaleesa had no one. "I'll tell you what. I'll be your friend, at least while I'm here. Deal?"

"Okay," Jaleesa said, brightening instantly.

"And maybe they just need to get to know you and see how cool you are."

"You think?"

"Of course, you're definitely cool. I'm sixteen years old, almost seventeen. Do you think I would hang around someone so much younger who wasn't cool?"

Jaleesa beamed proudly.

They continued walking and talking as Jaleesa showed her the main sights in Elwood—the movie theater, the museums, a couple of well-known clothing stores, schools, grocery stores and the mall. They passed a barber shop and beauty shop, then an antique store. Tamika paused a brief moment to glance at the window. They had all kinds of things, mostly like what she had in the attic and basement. She smiled, remembering what Lisa had said about finding treasure in her attic.

Jaleesa slowed, then stopped. "That's about it."

"So, what do you do around here for fun?"

Jaleesa shrugged and began walking her bike back toward the shopping mall area. "Some of the kids hang out over there."

"But you don't?"

"No," she said as she kept walking past the outside eatery.

Tamika checked out the small area beside the mall with the snack bar in front, seeing the girls who ignored them from earlier sitting at a picnic table out front. She noted their curious stares but just kept walking. She smiled to herself, knowing exactly what they were thinking. "Come on, let's go over and grab a drink or something."

"No, I can't," Jaleesa said.

"Of course you can. Come on, trust me," Tamika said as

she steered her bike across the street. Jaleesa finally followed. They parked their bikes beside a picnic table and ordered a soda. Tamika paid. They went back and sat down as the curious stares continued. With their heads close together they talked about Boston, then laughed and joked about living in a small town.

Tamika pulled out her MP3 player, turned the music up high, which was perfect for the two of them to hear along with anyone else close by. They started talking about high school and boyfriends and parties. It was obvious that Jaleesa was having fun and had completely forgotten the girls at the next table, who of course continued to listen in and stare.

Tamika told her one of the popular Boston witch stories as the table next to them went completely quiet. She knew the girls next to them were listening.

Eventually one of the girls at the next table called to Jaleesa. They started talking and then the other girls joined in. The tables merged as Tamika and Jaleesa took center stage talking about the Fourth of July party, music and high school.

Tamika joked with Jaleesa as though they had been best friends forever. The other girls seemed very impressed that she hung with older teens. One of them even asked Jaleesa to hang out with them at the mall the next day.

After a few more stories and much laughter, Tamika and Jaleesa got back on their bikes and headed back to Fraser.

"Thanks," Jaleesa said.

"For what?" Tamika asked.

Jaleesa smiled.

Tamika nodded. "You're welcome."

"We better get back. We can take a shortcut."

The shortcut turned out to be along a small river and over an old bridge. They paused and looked over at the water below.

"Guess what? Two people jumped off this bridge and died."

Tamika looked at Jaleesa. "When, lately?" she asked.

"No, it was a long time ago, way before I was born."

Tamika noticed that Jaleesa seemed particularly sad for some reason. "Did your family know them or were they related to you?"

"No, it just makes me sad, that's all. They just decided to jump. I can't imagine even thinking about doing something like that."

"Stay here," Tamika said, then hurried across the bridge with her camera. She started taking a few shots and realized that the light was perfect as it glistened off the water and reflected onto the bridge. When she finished she went back to where Jaleesa was still standing waiting.

"You like taking pictures?"

"Yeah."

"You should take pictures for my dad. He has all these pictures in his office. Want to see?"

"Sure," Tamika said, remembering their conversation about the house already being sold.

So the first stop when they got back to Fraser was Keith Tyler's office. As soon as they rode up, Tamika recognized the red car parked across the street. It wasn't too hard to figure out who her mother was having lunch with after that. She'd apparently had her late lunch with Keith Tyler.

Jaleesa and Tamika went into the real estate office, leaving the bikes outside. The place was deserted inside, only empty desks and chairs scattered around. "Come on. We can go into my dad's office and hang out. I'll show you his pictures," Jaleesa said, passing through.

"Where is everybody?"

"What everybody? Oh, you mean the employees?"

"Yeah, are they all out showing houses?"

"No, they're gone. Nobody works here anymore."

"But I thought your dad was like a big shot and had all this money and he knows all those rich people."

"That was before."

"Before what?"

"You won't tell him that I told you?" Jaleesa said.

Tamika leaned closer and shook her head.

"I heard my mom and dad talking. I think he's broke. Something about lawyer fees and court costs. Then my mom said that he bit off more than he could chew."

Tamika followed her to a large private office in the back. The sign on the door read Keith Tyler, III. Jaleesa barged right in. Tamika followed a bit more hesitantly. It was a typical office with a desk laden with a ton of books, two computers and dozens of rolled-up blueprints and photographs.

Tamika walked over to the photographs on the desk and side conference table. "So, what's all this for?" she asked, curiously looking at the photos.

"That's my dad's stuff. He has all these pictures of buildings and houses here and in Dallas and all over the country. He buys them. He's got tons. Sometimes he fixes them up and sometimes he just does nothing with them. But mostly he just buys them, at least before."

"Do you live with your dad?"

"Nah, I live here in town with my mom 'cause my dad mostly lives in Texas still. He comes here sometimes in the summertime. I visit him sometimes too. He used to have this humongous house with a swimming pool and a game room and all this other stuff."

"So what do you mean he fixes them up? To live in?"

"Nah, he has these people who are all over the place who fix up the houses and buildings so he can sell them again. I saw them doing it on television. I forget what it's called."

"You mean flipping?"

She shrugged and started laughing. "Oh, but one time during spring break when I was staying with my dad, he had to go to court 'cause he bought this house and the lady wanted it back."

"If he bought it, then how did she want it back?"

"I don't know. My mom told me that there was something in there that was worth a lot of money. He sold it someplace and got for-real cash. That's when the old owner wanted everything back and then she sued him."

"What happened?"

"Nothing at first. My dad already owned the house so nothing happened. He got to keep the house and everything in it. That lady was really pissed off. She used to stay over at my dad's house all the time before. I think she was his girlfriend," Jaleesa said, then leaned in and whispered, "They were having sex. I even heard them one time in his room. The whole house was rockin' they were so loud." She giggled. "So, anyway, after that, she kept calling my dad and yelling at him and cursing him out. She said that my dad used her, then dumped her. I don't know what happened after that 'cause my mom made me come back home."

"That's a shame," Tamika said, sympathizing with the lady who obviously fell for Keith's player bull.

"I know I was having a good time out there. Anyway, that was last year. Hopefully I can go visit him again this time without all the drama. But he had to get rid of his big house. Something about back taxes."

"Back taxes?"

"He owes the government a ton of cash from back when he played football. Here it is," she said as she handed Tamika a sold file. Tamika went through it. Jaleesa was right. Keith Tyler had sold a house that he didn't even own. There were inspections, appraisals and even a half-completed contract.

Tamika was just about to ask another question when her cell rang. She checked the number; it was Sean. She let the call go to missed calls, figuring that she'd call him back later. "I better get ready to go," she said.

"Was that your boyfriend?" Jaleesa asked.

"That was a friend," she corrected.

"A guy friend, right?" Jaleesa asked.

"Yes, Jaleesa, a guy friend."

"You like him a lot?"

"I don't know. Yeah, I guess so," she said, actually meaning it.

Jaleesa sighed dreamily. "I wish I was old enough to have a guy boyfriend. My mom said that I need to stop worrying about having a boyfriend and that most boys my age are mentally stunted. Do you think that's true?"

"Yeah, sometimes," Tamika said, thinking about Justin.

"But that's not fair. I think she's just saying that 'cause of my dad. They don't get along."

"Maybe, but you should listen to your mom. Believe me, you have plenty of time for all that. You'll find a guy who's perfect for you, mature and interesting. You'll see, just wait," she said, thinking about Sean.

"Yeah, I guess," Jaleesa relinquished. "You know, if my dad marries your mom we'd be stepsisters. He likes her."

"They're just old high school friends. Besides, my mom is married to my dad."

"Oh, that's no big deal. My mom was married to some-body else when she met my dad. She got divorced and they had me." Jaleesa went on to talk about something else, but Tamika was still focused on their last conversation. The idea of her mom getting divorced, then pregnant and hooking up with somebody like Keith Tyler was too horrible to imagine. It was time for her to get out of there.

After some quick directions from Jaleesa, Tamika was headed back to the house. Distracted, she'd been thinking about what Jaleesa said about her father buying up houses to flip, already selling her mom's house, and about his back taxes.

By the time she got back to the house she was excited to talk to her mother. The car was still gone but she went in calling out anyway. "Hello, Mom, I'm back." There was no answer so she headed directly to her laptop. Making the quick connection, she downloaded the bridge pictures. Pleased by what she saw, she began working, tweaking and altering with her filtering program. An hour later she had photos that were exceptional.

Since her mother still hadn't returned, Tamika decided to go back to Elwood. Remembering how she and Jaleesa had gone earlier, she got her camera and the ledgers with the letters, then went back to the antique shop in Elwood. She walked into the shop and was immediately helped by an older woman who introduced herself as Edna Hayes. Tamika talked to her about the house and showed her some of the digital pictures she'd taken.

"Some of these are really quite nice," Edna said. "And you said these are all in your attic and basement?"

"Yes, mostly."

"Where do you live in Elwood?"

"No, in Fraser. My name is Tamika Fraser."

"That's curious. Historically the man whom the town is named after had a son and his wife was named—"

"Tamika. Yes, I saw the grave in Alexandria."

"You saw it? How? Were you in Alexandria?"

"My mom, Laura Fraser, and I drove down from Boston and stopped to see it."

Edna flushed and chuckled. "That is remarkable. You're a descendent of the original family. You own the old Fraser home."

"Yes, at least that's what my mom said. I also brought a ledger and some letters that I thought might be interesting. I found them in an old rolltop desk." She pulled the book out of her backpack and flipped through several pages to the letters.

Edna read through the ledger and letters quickly. "My, these are very impressive indeed," she said, scanning the ledger and letters again. "These need to be authenticated."

"Okay, how do I do that?"

"I would presume your mother would handle that."

"She's a little busy at the moment. So I'm taking care of it. Do you do the authenticating here?"

"Yes, in most cases I am authorized to handle these things, but for these I'd like to get another eye."

"Meaning?"

"Meaning, if these are actual letters from that period, and I'm not saying that they are, they could be quite important."

"How important exactly?"

"The local historical museum burned down a few years ago, taking with it hundreds of original historical documents. They were each irreplaceable from the Fraser family archives. Only a few actually mentioned General Joseph Fraser. He was disowned by the family, so there was very little surviving information on him."

"Yes, I know the story. How long will it take to get them authenticated?"

"A few days, maybe up to two weeks, according to what we find out about them. I have a friend who works at the Historical Society library. I'm sure he'll be able to assist."

"Okay."

Edna took her name and phone number, then gave her a detailed receipt of the ledger and letters. "One more thing," Edna said. "Is this all?"

Tamika smiled, happy that she'd gone through and checked all the boxes. "No, there are Bibles and diaries and a few more ledgers and a lot more letters."

Edna beamed, barely able to control her excitement.

Tamika left feeling very pleased with herself.

chapter 18

Laura

Laura reached over with her fork and took a small piece of cheesecake. She put it in her mouth and let the rich, creamy goodness ease down her throat. "Hmm, you're right. Oh, man, that is sinfully delicious."

Keith, after sipping his coffee, licked his lips then smiled. "See, told you you'd love it."

"I do. Man, that is so good."

He chuckled. "I love watching you eat."

"Stop it," she said, playfully stealing another small forkful.

"Why don't I order you a slice?" he said as he looked around the restaurant for their waiter.

"No, no, really. I just wanted a small taste."

"Are you sure?" he asked.

She nodded.

"Thank you," he said.

"For what?" she asked.

"For this evening. You and me here tonight. Thank you. I'm glad you called me."

She blushed, slightly embarrassed by the truth. She had called him on impulse, then three minutes later wanted to change her mind. But she didn't.

"It was an impulse."

He smiled and raised his wineglass. "Here's to impulses."

Their glasses clinked. She sipped, then changed the subject. "So, when do you think we'll get rain again?"

He chuckled. "You know, you're something else."

"Me? Now, why would you say that?"

"Because you are. You're so incredible. You're intelligent, talented, fun to be with, beautiful, sexy, and I can't imagine being anywhere else right now." He reached over, took her hand and brought it to his lips. Kissing her gently, he looked up into her eyes. "Did I mention how incredibly beautiful and sexy you are this evening?"

Laura blushed. "Yes, I believe you did mention that."

"Sorry, it's just that you look so damn good this evening, so..." He paused as she looked away. "Sorry, did I embarrass you?"

"No," she lied softly. They looked into each other's eyes. She saw everything she thought she needed, wanted. The desire was there, the hunger, the want, but she still hung back.

"So, what did your daughter say when you told her that you had a date this evening?"

"First of all, this isn't a date. It's an evening out with an old friend. And second of all, I don't usually answer to my daughter."

"As to whether or not this is a date, I guess that's a matter of opinion. It is as far as I'm concerned. And as for your daughter, I get the feeling that she doesn't particularly care for me."

"She's a teenager, Keith. She doesn't particularly care for anyone. So, tell me about this business trip of yours."

"It's no big deal. I'm putting together the final investment proposals for my investors who'll be moving into the area. They're building an office complex and a shopping center not too far from here. I just have to pick up a few more loose ends and I'll be all set."

"That's right, you're in real estate. Sounds interesting, impressive."

"More like challenging."

"Yeah, I heard that," she said.

"Speaking of which, you know you still owe me a tour of your house. Is it on the market yet?"

"No, and believe me, you don't want to see that old place."

"Sure I do. It's something you're involved in so I'm interested. Now, what did you say you needed to get done?"

"There are dozens and dozens of boxes to go through— some to keep, others to just trash. My parents, grandparents and great-grandparents kept everything. The bedrooms, attic and basement are packed with things."

"What kind of things?" he asked curiously.

"All kinds of things—clothes, furniture, outdated electronics. There's a grandfather clock, jewelry, books, papers... Can you believe there's even a Victrola in the attic? I'm surprised there's not an Edsel somewhere in there." She chuckled and he joined in easily.

"There are also some ledgers and letters from the original Fraser family."

"Have you gotten them appraised?"

"No, not yet," she said.

"I wouldn't bother. I'm sure they're worthless."

"You think?" she asked, amazed by his statement.

"Sorry, but I see this kind of thing all the time. Don't get your hopes up."

"If you say so."

"Now, do you have a removal company yet?" he asked.

"No, we don't. We're not at that point yet. Tamika and I still have a lot of family mementos to go through."

"You know, since I am in real estate, I have a lot of connections. Maybe I can help out."

"How?"

"I'll buy the house and land sight unseen."

Laura started laughing. "No, no way. Nobody just up and buys a house they've never seen before."

"Why not, Laura? Look, I'm not trying to take anyone's business, but as a friend I need to tell you that you have to be careful. Not everyone has your best interests at heart. There're a lot of people out here, some with less than scrupulous ideas. I'll be happy to take the place off your hands intact as is."

"Are you serious?"

"Of course I am. Instead of dealing with all the cleaning out and stuff, I'll take it as is. I'll draw up the papers for you to sign and all this will be over."

"I don't know…"

"It's the best offer you're gonna get, I promise you. Or do the work, put in the needless hours and take your chances that someone will do me better, but I doubt it. Think about it, let me know."

She nodded and smiled. "Okay, thanks."

"Don't mention it. Now where were we? Ah yes, I remember," he said, then slid the dessert plate forward. Laura smiled as she picked up her fork again.

chapter 19

Tamika

"**Mom,** where are you?" Tamika called out excitedly after seeing her car parked out front.

"Down here," Laura called out from the basement.

"Guess what? I have incredible news." Tamika quickly cut through the kitchen and went down into the basement. Large and gloomy, it always seemed musty, damp and slightly chilly. "You're never gonna believe what I just did."

"We're over here."

Tamika walked over to her mom and Keith. They were sitting on one of the old sofas with dozens of books and boxes laid out around them. "Hey, sweetie," Laura said, handing Keith another book.

"Hi, Mom."

"Tamika, you remember Mr. Tyler from the Fourth of July party."

Tamika half smiled.

"He wanted to see the inside of the house. He thinks he

might be able to get us a good price on it, plus clear out a lot of these old things."

"Hello, Tamika. How've you been?" Keith asked.

"Hi," she said, then paused.

"So, what's this exciting news?" Laura asked.

"It's no big deal, I can tell you later," Tamika said, then turned to leave.

"Uh, listen, I have to get going anyway," Keith said. "Thanks for the tour. This is truly a remarkable house. Think about what I said. I'm serious. I'll be happy to take care of everything for you."

"Thanks, Keith. I'll walk you out."

Laura walked Keith upstairs and to the front door, then turned to see Tamika standing waiting for her. "So, okay, what's the incredible news you have for me?"

Tamika paused, realizing that she wasn't as excited anymore. "Nothing, just that I found some ledgers in the attic. Did you ever get them appraised?"

Laura shrugged. "I think my grandmother did that once. I remember my mother talking about it. The appraiser wanted to buy them, but he told her that they were basically worthless."

"Historical value alone, they could be priceless."

"Historical value?" Laura questioned, slightly impressed. "Since when are you interested in historical value? For that matter, since when are you interested in history?"

"Have you seen those letters?"

"Not lately."

"They're amazing. They talk about the Civil War and slavery and all kinds of old stuff. And one of the ledgers has a roll call of the property they owned—cows, land, buildings and slaves. The names of the slaves in it included birth dates and dates of death, children and everything. It's amazing. You should see some of the entries."

"So, what are you saying? You want to get them appraised?"

"Yeah, I think it's a good idea," Tamika said, omitting the part that she'd already taken them into the antique shop in town.

"Fine, do it."

"Are you serious?"

"Of course, they're yours too. You're part of the Fraser family. That makes them yours as well."

"Okay," Tamika said.

"Sounds like you're turning into a history buff," Laura said as she began flipping through the mail on the foyer table.

"I wouldn't say all that. It's just interesting since it's about our family."

"Like the cemeteries?" Laura asked, looking up.

Tamika yielded and nodded. "Yeah, okay, like the cemeteries."

Laura nodded, then handed Tamika a card. "Another postcard from your dad."

"So, what was he doing here?" Tamika asked, following her mom into the kitchen.

Laura smiled. "Keith and I had an early dinner in town and he wanted to see the inside of the house. Since he's in real estate he suggested that he might be able to help us out."

"How? What kind of help? I thought we were selling the house on our own, not with a Realtor company. For real, wasn't that the whole idea of having a specialist come over? Speaking of which, she came by earlier after you left."

"She came by? What happened? What did she say?"

"I think she had some good ideas. She gave me this."

Tamika handed her a sheet of paper she'd been given along with her added notes. Laura glanced over it quickly.

"Paint, clean, trash, garden, okay." She looked at Tamika. "Wow, this is a lot to do. What do you think? Can we get all this done?"

"No," Tamika said. Laura sighed heavily, assuming that Tamika was still in her mood. "There's no way we can clean this whole place and paint everything by ourselves—not without help—so I got these." She pulled a couple of business cards out of her pocket.

"What are these?"

"I stopped by the hardware store when I was in Elwood. I got some paint samples and some business cards. We can get one of these companies to paint the outside and inside, then have a cleaning service come in to finish up stuff we can't do like refinish the wood floors. All we have to do is go through the family boxes and personal stuff."

Laura smiled. That was exactly what she'd planned. "Sounds great in theory, but it's still a lot of work, not to mention expensive," she said, looking at, then shuffling the business cards.

"I guess we can paint the inside of the house and maybe get one of those big trash containers and just start pulling stuff out."

Laura nodded. "Or maybe, I guess we can just turn it over and let someone else bother with it."

"Turn it over to who?"

"Whom," she corrected. "Keith."

"I thought we were selling it ourselves."

"I know, but maybe he could do better for us."

"What do you mean?"

"Well, he saw all this stuff we have lying around and offered to help."

"How exactly?" Tamika asked.

"He offered to buy the house as is, everything still inside."

"What? No way."

"We won't have to do anything."

"Did you say yes already?"

"No, I didn't," Laura said as Tamika sighed her relief. "Although I didn't say no either. This place eats up a lot of cash in taxes and upkeep. The property rates have gone up, thanks to new growth in Elwood. People are starting to find Fraser again."

"Still, we don't have to sell it to him."

"He does this for a living. He takes abandoned buildings and old homes off the owners' hands. So basically he cleans out old houses all the time, trashes everything, guts them, then puts them back on the market. It's a service he offers."

"And what does he get out of it?"

"He helps people."

"He told you that?"

"Yes."

"You believe him?"

"What kind of question is that? Of course I believe him. Why wouldn't I?"

"Oh, I don't know, 'cause he's lying."

"Tamika!"

"So that's what he wants to do with our house."

"It's a possibility, yes, and working with him you'll get back to Boston that much sooner. All I have to do is sign a contract and he'll take care of everything. We just pack up whatever we brought down and drive off. That's what you wanted, right?"

"I don't think that's a good idea."

"Why not? You wanted to get back home to Boston."

"I know but maybe you should know more about what he does before you sign anything."

"He's willing to take care of everything, and to tell you the truth, I'm just about settled on letting him do it. That way I don't have to think about it or make any decisions. I'm so sick of being responsible, of making decisions—what to cook for dinner, where to go on vacation, how many, how much, what, when, where, how—I'm sick of it," she ranted.

"Okay, fine, I'll make the decisions. I'll take care of everything. Just give me your credit card," Tamika said. Laura looked at her as if she were crazy. "Mom, I'm serious. You're always talking about me stepping up so I'm doing it now. So let me."

"You want me to hand over my credit card to you?"

"Yes, and before you say anything, I won't be going on any shopping sprees like before."

"You mean when you used the emergency credit card and threw a party at the house with your boyfriend?"

"That was before and, yes, I'm serious. I can do this. I want to do this. I'll write up a budget, get quotes and take care of everything. All you have to do is say yes."

Laura looked at her and shook her head skeptically. "Well?" Tamika encouraged.

"I'll think about it, okay?" she said. Tamika nodded. "So, what are you up to now?"

"Nothing. I just got in and I wanted to—"

"That's right, I almost forgot. You mentioned Elwood. You went there today?"

"Yeah, Jaleesa took me over."

"Jaleesa?"

"Your friend's daughter from the other night."

"Oh, right. How did you get there? I know she's not driving at her age."

"I took the bike from the garage," Tamika said.

"So, what did you think of it?"

"It's nice. A lot bigger than Fraser definitely. It's like a small city, way bigger than I thought."

"That's for sure. So, what did you think of Fraser?"

"It's small, kinda empty. But when I was in Keith Tyler's office he had all these plans and pictures of proposed buildings and—"

"Wait a minute. What were you doing in Keith's office?"

"He wasn't there, but I guess you know that already. I was there with Jaleesa."

"Really?"

"Anyway, he has all these pictures in his office. Did you know that he's in the middle of this huge court case about taxes and he had some kind of foreclosure company that had been cheating people and taking the equity out of their property?"

"What? Where did you hear that?"

"I read it online."

"You found out about a tax problem online?"

"No, Jaleesa told me that part. Her mother told her—well, maybe more like she overheard them talking about it."

"You spied on him?" she asked.

"No, I talked with his daughter, then went online. I can't help it if his own daughter talks, and whatever's written online is in the public domain. That means anybody is free to check it out. Good or bad, it's there."

"Okay, fine, but going into his office was…"

"It's not like I broke in. Jaleesa took me. She wanted to show me the pictures of the houses he has. Did you know that he was in the middle of maybe trying to buy this house from Grandma and he maybe even sold this house already?"

"Maybe? What do you mean? What are you talking about?"

"I can't prove it but he has a file and pictures of our house dated back before Grandma died. There was a half-done contract and everything. He sold the house already."

"Tamika, you went into his files?"

"Jaleesa let me see them. He's broke, Mom, and he's trying to scam you."

"What?"

"Jaleesa told me that he and her mom argue all the time 'cause he doesn't pay child support and she had to go back to work and even gives him money."

"It makes him a jerk, not broke. Tamika, I've seen his car, his jewelry, his clothes. There's no way he's broke."

"I think he's fronting."

"Tamika, I think that since you don't care for him you're probing just to find something."

"I can't help it if it's already out there."

"I'm seriously considering turning the house over to him."

"You can't. You always say that you know better and that I can't see things clearly because I'm only sixteen. Well, I see exactly what he's up to. You can't see it because you like him. You always want me to trust you when it comes to my boyfriends. Well, it's your turn to trust me. I see him like you saw Justin. They're both losers and users."

"Tamika…"

"Mom."

"Okay, enough. Let's just agree not to agree," she said, then walked away, leaving Tamika to consider her comments.

Tamika sat in the dining room stewing. There was no way she was wrong about Keith Tyler. He was a user. Yes, she wanted to go back home but she also wanted to do the right thing. And when it came to her mother's new friend, something just didn't seem right.

Thinking more about what she'd read and what Jaleesa said about her dad, Tamika wondered exactly what he was up to. Going back online, she started checking out the Tyler Real Estate Web site again. But just as the home page came up she saw that Sean was online so she sent an IM.

Tamika: Hey, u there
Sean: yeah, hi
Tamika: I called U
Sean: I was busy, I called back
Tamika: I know, I missed U'R call
Tamika: I thought U were avoiding me

She waited, but he didn't respond.

Tamika: Sorry about B4. I was pissed. My mom is driving me crazy. I don't know what 2 do anymore. She's so blind when it comes 2 certain people. I keep telling her they frontin' and she just ignores me. She's driving me crazy!!

He didn't respond again.

Tamika: R U there
Sean: yeah

Tamika continued typing her rant about her mother then stopped and deleted it, deciding to change the subject.

Tamika: I took U'R advice
Sean: ?
Tamika: checking out Fraser
Sean: finally
Tamika: yeah, I know

He didn't respond for a while.

Tamika: R U busy?

He still didn't respond.

Tamika: R U OK?
Sean: U like it?
Tamika: like what?
Sean: Fraser
Tamika: it's okay, I guess—I was taking pictures
Sean: of what?
Tamika: Fraser
Sean: LOL, really?
Tamika: yeah, it's not so bad. I saw this old bridge
not far from here. Somebody told me that 2 people died
jumping off
Sean: I know the bridge—they died back N the day
Tamika: I wonder Y?
Sean: I'll tell U about it L8R
Tamika: promise??
Sean: yeah
Tamika: missed u on the 4th
Sean: things got messed up, couldn't make it.

Tamika looked at his response. She was surprised that she was more upset and disappointed than she thought she would be.

Tamika: maybe next time
Sean: U saw Fraser where else?
Tamika: I went 2 this place called Elwood
Sean: really? that's where my grandparents live
Sean: that's where I'm staying
Tamika: I was there 2day, it's nice
Sean: I gotta show u around
Tamika: okay
Sean: so what R U up 2 2nite?
Tamika: nothing, U?
Sean: driving around
Tamika: how's Boston?
Sean: okay, I guess

There was an e-mail arrival signal. Tamika split the page and read the mail. It was from Edna Hayes at the Elwood Antique Shop. She wrote that she'd taken the ledger and letters to her friend at the museum and they were very interested in seeing more samples. Tamika squealed, she was so thrilled.

Tamika: I GTG
Sean: ok L8R

She signed off, excited to tell her mother about the antique shop request. Laura was in the kitchen with the refrigerator and freezer wide open. "So, what do you want for dinner tonight?"

"I thought you already had your dinner date."

"It wasn't a dinner date We ate dinner, that's all. I know, how about if I take you out this evening? We went to this great restaurant and they have the best cheesecake I've ever tasted." She turned around smiling. "How about dinner out tonight?"

"Yeah, why not?" Tamika said, then went upstairs to get ready to go.

Laura stepped out on the porch just as a young man walked up the stone path. "May I help you?" she asked.

"Hi, Mrs. Fraser?"

"Yes, and you are?"

"My name's Sean Edwards. I'm a friend of Tamika's from Boston."

"Boston? You came all the way down here from Boston?"

"No, ma'am, I'm visiting my grandparents. They live in Elwood. Tamika and I go to school together, though."

"Really?" Laura said. "Tamika's upstairs. She'll be right down. But to tell you the truth we're on our way out to dinner."

"Oh, well, I guess I can come back later."

"No, no, why don't you join us for dinner?"

"I don't want to impose, ma'am."

"You wouldn't be imposing, it's an invitation. I'm sure Tamika will be delighted to have a friend from Boston to talk to."

"Okay, thanks," he agreed.

"Why don't you have a seat? She'll be down shortly." He sat down and they continued talking.

After changing, Tamika came down the stairs and headed to the front door. Even before opening the screen she heard her mother laughing and talking. Figuring she was on the phone or had one of her friends over, she opened the door but stopped in her tracks. "What are you doing here?"

chapter 20

Laura

The following week and a half whipped by in a flash. Laura's friend, Grace, was still away on business, so she spent just about every day hanging out with Keith. Sleeping most mornings, she hung out afternoons and evenings into the early-morning hours. Day trips, movies, shopping, horse races, dinner, parties—she was having a blast.

The new outfits she bought and new hairstyle had done the trick—she felt fantastic. Stretching leisurely, she ran her fingers through her short hair. It felt different but she liked it. The pixie haircut was something she'd done on impulse. She got up and went to the mirror, turning her face from side to side. It made her look years younger, as did her old wardrobe, or rather her new old wardrobe.

As soon as she turned to head to the bathroom, her cell rang. She answered, "Hello."

"Woman, I know you must have had a damn good reason for missing my welcome-back birthday celebration."

Laura chuckled. Grace had had six birthday celebrations

since she arrived a little over a month ago. "Welcome back, stranger. Sorry, I had a dinner engagement."

"Girl, please don't tell me you're still swinging on that man's arm. You know he only wants one thing from you."

"You know, I thought so too, but really, he's pretty nice. We talk and he just listens."

"Lordy, it's more serious than I thought. The man is downright dangerous. He's listening. Girl, you know he's up to no good now."

Laura laughed. "Oh, come on, Gracie. Give him a break. He's really nice once you get to know the real man."

"And you have?"

"Yes, I have," Laura assured her. "I know him."

"Said the fly of the spider," Grace muttered.

"Gracie, for real, nothing's happening. He hasn't even tried to kiss me."

"Honey, he can get sex from anyone. You've got something else he wants. But okay, okay, I know when to butt out and keep my mouth shut. I just want you to be careful. But funny, I remember telling you this exact same thing about two dozen years ago, or have you forgotten that tutoring fiasco?"

"He was young then, so was I. I know better now."

"Do you? Do you really? Lordy, a smooth-talking man is a smooth-talking man, period, no matter how old."

"Gracie…"

"But as I said, I know when to butt my nose out. So how's the house coming along?"

"Girl, you wouldn't believe the place now. It looks incredible. When the Realtor specialist stopped by the other day she was amazed by the change. I have to admit Tamika has really put her heart into getting it together. I was really apprehensive and skeptical about giving her my credit card, but she's been seriously great. She's even trying to schedule an estate auction and then a yard sale in a few weeks."

"For real?"

"Oh yeah, she's serious. I've never seen her so focused. She's plastered, painted, sanded the floors and heaven knows what else. She even got one of those storage bins that can be shipped intact."

"Fantastic. I should get her to organize around here."

"Seriously, the place looks incredible. She even got a friend of hers, Sean, from Boston to give her a hand with the painting."

"Sean—that's her boyfriend?"

"She says that they're just friends, but I don't know. I think there's more. At least he's better than that guy she used to hang with, Justin. He was out-and-out using her and she didn't even see it. But I like Sean, he seems like a really nice guy."

"Well, I'm glad for both of you. So listen. The reason I called is to ask if you've considered that article I talked to you about a while ago. The editor I work with is really interested."

"Actually, I have been thinking about it and I have an idea that I'd like to explore. So what exactly do I have to do? Submit samples of my writing, a synopsis or ideas?"

"You can do a pitch first, then send an outline. I'll get you the e-mail address."

"Can I ask one favor?"

"Sure, what?"

"I haven't seriously written in years and I have a feeling you hyped me up too much. Would you look at the piece before I send it out?"

"Sure, no problem."

"Okay, great," Laura said, relieved.

"I'm so excited about this. Why don't I conference-call

my editor and get back to you this afternoon? You can pitch her then."

"Sounds good, and thank you, Gracie."

"What are friends for? But listen, I gotta go. I'm on deadline and my article is still rough. Talk to you later."

Laura hung up feeling even better if that was possible. Her mind was alight and her thoughts blazed with ideas. Having not written a serious piece in years, she knew she'd enjoy the challenge. She quickly showered, dressed, then headed downstairs to get started.

As soon as she stepped into the kitchen she saw the laptop computer on the table, perfect placement. Assuming that Tamika was either still asleep or in her bedroom on her cell, Laura decided to borrow her laptop to jot down a few notes for the conference call and outline.

When she turned it on and saw the screen saver she was amazed. It was a photo taken during their drive down of the two of them in the car. But this photo was astonishing. She knew Tamika loved taking pictures and was good, but she had no idea she was this talented. She opened the screen saver settings and the My Pictures file and reviewed the other photos. Some of them were extraordinary.

She grabbed her cell and called Grace again. After a brief conversation she hung up and called her husband. As usual she left a message; he was unavailable. She hadn't actually spoken to him in days and even then it was just a two-minute conversation. He was in the middle of something and couldn't talk, it was in the middle of the night and he was tired or she just couldn't get through—either way, she was tired of playing phone tag.

Motivated by the photos, she excitedly typed a few ideas outlining the basic direction she hoped to go with the article.

Satisfied, she elaborated more. An hour later she'd written a ten-page article inspired by her daughter's work. She went back to the first page and added her byline, by Laura Fraser, photos by Tamika Fraser. She dropped the article outline into an e-mail along with several selected pictures, then sent them out.

"Hey," Tamika said, standing in the open doorway, "what's up?"

"I am, believe it or not. Good morning."

"You're using the laptop?" Tamika asked, surprised.

"Yes, I had a few ideas I wanted to write down."

"What kind of ideas?"

"I'll let you know in a few. So, what are your plans today?"

"I have to check on something so I need a ride to Elwood."

Laura stood, walked over to the counter drawer and grabbed a set of keys inside. "Here," she said, handing Tamika the keys.

"What are these to?"

"Keys to the car out front."

"Aunt Sylvia's car?"

"Actually, it's my car, or rather the car my mother left me along with the house."

"That's your car outside?" Tamika asked.

Laura nodded.

"That's why you rented a car to drive down here so that you could drive that car back, right?"

"Something like that."

"So I get to drive the car now?" she asked hopefully.

"You get to use the car today to go to Elwood. That's as far as it goes."

"Cool." She relented easily. "So, what's for breakfast?"

"Let's go out for breakfast."

A few minutes later, each having driven separately, Laura and Tamika sat at an outside table at Mrs. Oliver's Bakery eating bagels and cheese and drinking hot tea and iced coffee. "You know, this was our place to hang out when I was your age."

"A bakery? You hung out at a bakery?" Tamika said.

"Yeah, we didn't have malls like you have now back then."

"You mean back in the Stone Age?" she joked.

"Yeah, I was sitting right here when they invented the wheel," Laura played along. "But anyway, Grace, Judy, Fran and I used to come here after school."

"I thought you said that you had to go straight home after school."

"Well, we kind of invented this club and I told my mom I was the president and once a week we had a meeting."

"You were president?"

"Technically we were all president and irreplaceable as far as each of our parents was concerned. So when we had a meeting we had to be there."

"So that's what you did to hang out?" Tamika asked. Laura nodded. "It sounds extreme."

"It was and at the time it was brilliant. At least we thought so."

"So, where did Keith Tyler come in?"

"He didn't."

"But didn't you tutor him or something?"

"Where did you get that?"

"Just guessing," Tamika lied.

"You know I don't believe that," Laura said. Tamika shrugged, then waited for her mother to continue. "Keith was one of the cool kids. His dad owned a huge business, he had money and just about every girl in school had a crush on him. I, on the other hand, was just a regular student. He and his friends had cars and hung out at the movie theater in Elwood. Me and my friends hung out here."

"And you had a crush on him?" Tamika said.

Laura looked at her daughter, surprised by the remark. "What makes you say that? Where are you getting these ideas?"

"I kinda read your diary."

"My diary," she said, then paused in understanding. "Oh, right, I'd forgotten all about them. Wait, there was no way you could have gotten that just from reading one diary."

Tamika smiled. "I read a couple."

"A couple?"

"All of them," she finally confessed.

"And?" Laura asked.

"And they were confusing, at least at first."

"That was the whole idea. You need the key to get the right order in order to understand it."

"What's the key?"

"I'm not gonna tell you."

"Why not? Mom, you wrote those, what, over thirty-five years ago, so what's the big deal?"

"It has not been over thirty-five years and the big deal is that nobody was supposed to read and understand them, not even my dear nosy daughter."

"One thing I didn't get. I know Aunt Deb died back then but what happened to her daughter?"

"Aunt Sylvia adopted her and raised her as her own."

"That would make Cousin Roberta my cousin Roberta?" Tamika said. Laura nodded. "Actually, I did understand them mostly, kinda. They were interesting. I learned a lot about you."

"Really, did you? What did you learn?" Laura asked.

"Mainly that I'm a lot like my mother."

"Funny, I remember saying that same thing not too long

ago." She laughed, and Tamika joined in. "Okay, so you may know one of my little secrets. Now it's your turn."

"What?"

"You and Sean?"

"Are just friends."

"Justin?"

"History."

"Good. I like Sean. He's nice, he's cute."

"Yeah, so you've said about a hundred times. Don't you know you're not supposed to say that? It's the kiss of death to have a parent approve of a guy."

"Whatever. The point is Sean seems genuinely nice."

"Like Dad nice?"

"Yeah."

"Talk about the kiss of death," Tamika said.

"Hey, y'all." Both Laura and Tamika looked up. "Girl, I was just about to call you."

"Hey, Gracie," Laura said, smiling up at Grace as she dragged a chair over and sat beside her.

"Hi," Tamika said, standing. "Mom, I gotta go. I need to take care of something before the outside painters come by to finish up the trim and before Sean comes by."

"Sean?" Grace asked, smiling.

"He's a friend, that's all," Tamika said, smiling. "Y'all two are just alike. See you at home later, Mom. Bye, Ms. Hunter."

"Okay, drive safe."

"I will," Tamika said as she headed to the car parked beside her mother's rental.

"Impressive, you letting Tamika drive. The last time you—"

"Yeah, yeah, I know, but she's really matured. I trust her and I'm really proud of her."

"It shows. Speaking of which, I read your article outline, then sent it on to my editor."

"And?" Laura asked hopefully.

"She loved it, the whole concept. Girl, she raved. I think this could really be something for you."

"Really? Seriously, you liked it? She liked it?"

"Loved it is more accurate. It's warm and genuine without being preachy. Perfect for the magazine's format. I'm thinking possibly of running a series."

"Whoa, I don't know about all that."

"Think about it. It's not out of the question."

"Man, this is crazy. I never expected anything like this to happen."

"It's time to celebrate."

"Yeah," Laura said, "and I know just what to do."

"What?" Grace asked excitedly.

"Remember when we spent the night in the high school?"

"You mean when we broke into the high school?"

"Semantics."

"You're not thinking about doing that again, are you?"

"Yeah, why not?"

"Are you crazy? Once was enough."

"Come on, it'll be fun. Your kids are grown, Tamika's a teenager. She's almost done with the house, the summer's almost over and I'll be leaving soon. What about it? One last hurrah, something to remember again?"

"Yeah, an arrest record is definitely something to remember all right. Fingerprints, photos—nah, I don't think so. Hanging out till dawn is one thing. Getting charged and going to county is another," Grace said.

"We won't get charged if we're not caught. We did it before, we can do it again."

"And what makes you think we won't get caught? The school probably has an alarm system, motion detectors and ray guns and who knows what else? What makes you think it's gonna be as easy as last time?"

Laura chuckled at the ray gun remark. "Same as before, the place is huge. If the police come in one door we simply go out the other or we just hide until they leave. They'll never find us."

Grace paused to think about it. "I don't know. It sounds too risky. We're grown women now, not teenagers."

"That's exactly the point. Teenagers have all the fun. I think it's time that we have a little bit of that fun too."

"Sounds like you're overdoing it."

"Not at all. I'm just finally enjoying myself," Laura said, seeing Grace's mind racing through the possibilities.

"Tell you what. You get Francine and Judith on board and I'm there too."

"Great."

"So, when do you want to do this caper, Ms. Catwoman?"

"No time like the present."

"Uh-uh, no way. At least do it at night like before."

"Okay, good, fine, tonight. I'll call you later to come up with a meeting place. We'll bring the same things as before."

"All right," Grace said cautiously. "I gotta go and get this article in before we go to jail for life."

"Don't be so negative. We'll be fine," Laura said as a tingle of excitement shivered through her. It felt incredible, as if she were finally alive after so long. She sat back in the chair considering what they should do.

First things first, she made a couple more calls relaying the same message and having the same reluctant conversation. Then, finally getting all four of her friends on board, she planned the details.

By that evening, dressed in jeans and dark T-shirts, with backpacks and sleeping bags, Laura, Grace, Judith and Francine walked through the front door at Fraser High School exactly as they did over twenty years ago.

Flashlights gleamed off the walls as the four walked through the darkened hallway. "I can't believe we're doing this again," Grace said excitedly as they started walking around.

"Come on, let's check out the gym," Laura said. They followed. She opened the doors, walked in and stood in the center of the hardwood floor. "Wow, look at this place," she said, shining the light in the darkness. "Doesn't it bring back memories?" Suddenly the overhead lights came on. They all looked around as Judith continued pushing buttons.

Francine picked up a basketball sitting on the bleachers and tossed it at the basket. They all booed when she missed. After a few minutes they were teamed up playing a make-shift game with sneakers squeaking and them giggling. Grace found a jump rope, prompting them to all join in. Laughing and exhausted, they finally left, continuing to the cafeteria down the hall.

Laura pulled out brown sack lunches from her backpack and after a treat of bologna-and-cheese sandwiches, chocolate pudding, chips and ginger ale, they sat in the school's cafeteria laughing and talking about their lives.

"I never thought it would be so hard," Judith said.

"Seriously, my mom made it look easy. I can't imagine raising seven kids like she did," Francine added.

"As babies and toddlers they're cool. It's when they get older, teenagers…" Laura said.

"Girl, you ain't lying about that," Grace said.

"Thank God mine are still young," Francine added.

"Not for long," they all replied jokingly.

"How on earth did you manage to raise two teenage boys alone without losing your mind?" Laura asked Grace, whose children were the oldest of all of them.

"Who said I didn't lose my mind? Of course I did," Grace said. They laughed. "You get used to it. The hardest part is dealing with attitude."

"Hear, hear, I have a tween and a fifteen-year-old and they both drive me nuts. I threaten to walk away and never come back daily. And you know what? Sometimes I actually feel like doing just that," Judith confessed.

"Sure you do. We all do," Laura said.

"Who doesn't?" Grace agreed. "My teenage son wanted his ear pierced and my other teenage son wanted a tattoo."

"Did you get it for them?" Laura asked.

"Hell no, but damned if he didn't get a tattoo when he went away to college. Fraternities of course."

"I always wanted a tattoo," Laura said.

"Me too."

"I was too chicken."

"I heard that."

"We should do it now."

"Do what?"

"Get a tattoo."

"Yeah, right."

The four women looked at each other, then burst out laughing, knowing that there was no way it was going to happen. They stood and gathered the last bits of dinner, then headed off to continue their tour of the building, classrooms, library, administrative office and then finally to the main auditorium.

They went up onstage. Grace switched on the lights.

Francine turned on the CD player. Laughing, joking around and dancing, they enjoyed themselves as memories flooded back. "Remember this dance?" Francine said.

"Oh yeah, how about this?" Laura said.

"The running man, I could never do that."

The freedom continued until Laura misstepped, slipped and tumbled off the stage. She braced herself, falling face-first.

chapter 21

Tamika

spackling, plastering and painting, as usual, had taken up most of their afternoon. Then after a quick break for a late lunch they finished up later in the evening with touch-ups and tape removal. They were cleaning up for the day while drinking sodas and talking.

"You know, this place looks awesome," Sean said, looking around at the walls they'd just painted.

"You think?" Tamika said, following his lead as she pulled blue cover tape from the white baseboard trim.

He nodded. "You did a serious job, for real."

"*We* did a serious job," she corrected.

"Nah, I came in at the end and besides, I just did what I was told. You did all this. Girl, you bad."

Tamika smiled and nodded. "It does look pretty good, doesn't it? You know what, it actually looks like something my mom would do. I can't believe it. Funny, I used to think that there was no way I was like her. Looks like I was wrong."

"What's so bad about being like your mom?"

"Are you kidding? Everything," she immediately said, then changed her mind. "Well, maybe not everything."

"Your mom's cool."

Tamika shook her head. "Cool isn't exactly what I'd call her. She's so different being down here. It's like she gave up on being what she was."

"What was she?" he asked.

"She was responsible, in charge, she did things."

"Sounds more like you now, doesn't it?"

"Ugh, I'm turning into my mother. Great," she said. Sean laughed, and Tamika smiled.

"So, what's your mom doing tonight?" he asked.

"Hanging out, I guess, as usual. I don't know what's gotten into her. Suddenly she's gone hangout nuts. She's obsessed with her high school crush and she's acting like she's sixteen years old all over again."

Sean started laughing again.

"Oh, you think that's funny?" Tamika asked.

"No, no," he said, still chuckling. "I'm just saying for real you sound just like my grandmom talking or rather complaining around the house."

"Thanks a lot. I'm turning into my mother and sounding like your grandmother." They chuckled. "But seriously," she protested, "I'm just making sense. This guy she's hanging with is nothing but trouble."

"So tell her."

"I did, I do, constantly. She's just not listening as usual. My dad at least listens halfway. That is, when he's not busy working. For real, please tell me your mom and dad aren't crazy like this."

"My mom and dad aren't crazy like this," he repeated

exactly, then laughed. She swatted at his arm but he moved away too quickly.

"Ha-ha, not funny. So what about your mom and dad?"

"What about them?" he asked, then paused a moment before elaborating. "I live with my dad and my stepmom, so as far as moms go, she all right, I guess. She's cool."

"Where's your real mom?" she asked as she picked up the massive cotton tarp covering the floor.

"Actually, she is my real mom," Sean said as he grabbed the other end and started helping her fold the large cloth. "She raised me since I was a baby, so that's real enough for me. She's the only mom I know. My birth mother gave me up and just walked away. My dad took me, got married and that was it."

"Wow, I didn't know," she said, meeting him to gather the ends together.

"For real, no big deal, it happens."

"Don't you ever wonder about her?"

"Nah, I have a great family—my dad, my mom, my grand-parents, uncles, aunts and a ton of cousins."

"You have any brothers or sisters?" she asked.

"My stepmom can't have kids so there were always foster kids around. Not so much now."

"Wow, that's so cool. You're lucky."

"Yeah, I think so too. But check, so are you. Your mom's cool. She, like, handed you a credit card and just let you do all this on your own. That's tight."

Tamika nodded, then stepped back to check out the room again. She turned completely around. "For real, this place looks incredible. I can't believe it. We did this. It's like a whole new house now. Thanks for helping."

"For real, I ain't do nothing. You did most of this by yourself," Sean said approvingly as he looked around.

Tamika smiled, looking around. He was right; she'd done most of this all by herself. She called people, organized, hired companies and even in one case dismissed a company that wanted to overcharge her before even starting the job.

"So what's next?" he asked.

"This was the last room to get painted. The guys are coming tomorrow to finish the wood floors and to paint the outside trim. The yard sale is the day after that."

"Are you ready for all that?"

"Sure," she said nonchalantly, then, noticing his expression, continued. "Why wouldn't I be?"

"You were talking about your mom being different down here. So are you."

"I'm not different," she protested.

"Yeah, I mean in school you're hanging around your friends and Justin and—"

"Yeah, Justin, whatever," she said, dismissing the conversation. "So, ninth grade, huh?"

"What about it?"

"You for real wanted my phone number, huh?" She smirked slyly.

Sean looked at her, and his expression softened. "Yeah, but you were all into your world so I had to let that go."

"I was not all into my world, but I was into my studies if that's what you mean. I was trying to get good grades."

"Uh-huh, hanging with Justin."

"Nah, I was, for real. But I remember you were all into football and hanging with Lexea." He laughed. "Nah, nah, don't be playing it off. Y'all guys are all alike with that stuff."

"Nah, not all guys. Lexea is played out for real."

"Yeah, right."

"For real," he insisted. "I can't deal with her drama."

"Whatever," Tamika said. "So, when are you leaving?"

"You trying to get rid of me already?"

"No," she said truthfully.

"Day after tomorrow," he said. They each went quiet.

"It was cool having you down here," she said.

"Yeah," he said, taking her hand, "thanks."

Tamika leaned in and kissed him sweetly. He kissed her back. Afterward he smiled as she looked away.

"You kissed me," he said.

"Yeah," she said, "I had to."

"Why do you say that?"

"Well, since it took you two years to get my phone number I figured it would take you at least four years to kiss me, so…" she said, smiling. He laughed just as her cell phone rang. She grabbed it off the chair and answered.

"Hi, Tamika, this is Edna Hayes. I'm calling from the—"

"Yes, I remember, hi. Did you find anything out?"

"Actually I did. I took the pieces over to the Historical Society at the museum and they were very impressed."

"That's good, right?"

"Actually it's very good," Edna said.

"Really? So the letters and the ledger are real?"

"Yes, they're genuine. I think I should speak to your mother at this point. We have a few questions for her."

"She's not in at the moment. I can have her call you."

"That would be great. Please tell her that I have been authorized to make an offer of behalf of the museum."

"An offer?" Tamika said, beaming, then listened as Edna went on to tell her things she mostly already knew. They ended the conversation with Edna asking for her to come into the store as soon as possible. Tamika hung up, excited, then called her mother's cell. There was no answer.

"What's up?" Sean asked.

"I need to find my mom."

"Do you know where she is?" he asked.

"Kind of. I'm going over to her friend's house. Hopefully she's there."

"Want a ride?"

"Nah, I got the car outside."

"You got a car?" he asked.

"It's a long story. Come on, let's go."

As soon as they stepped outside on the porch, Sylvia was coming up the front steps. "Aunt Sylvia, hi. I didn't know you were coming today," Tamika said.

"Thought I'd stop by and see how you two were getting along. And who is this young man?"

"Aunt Sylvia, this is Sean, my friend from Boston. Sean, this is my great-aunt Sylvia."

"Hello, ma'am," he said politely, reaching out to shake her hand.

"A friend, huh?"

"Yes," they both said instantly.

"One of those friends with privileges?" she asked.

"Aunt Sylvia!" Tamika said, stunned by her frankness.

"No, ma'am, just friends," Sean said quickly, blushing.

"I'm just asking," Sylvia said innocently. "Where are y'all off to so rushed?"

"Looking for Mom. I took a ledger and some letters from the attic to the Elwood Antique Shop. They want to make an offer but I need Mom and she's not answering her cell. I need to find her."

"Do you know where she is?"

"No, I'm gonna go by Ms. Hunter's house. Hopefully she's over there. She told me that they're supposed to be hanging out tonight. Want to come?"

"Sure, why not?" Sylvia said. After saying goodbye to Sean they got in the car and drove off. "So, are you interested in selling the letters?"

"I don't know. Whatever Mom wants to do, I guess."

"What about you? Do you think they should be sold?"

"No, probably not, but we can't just leave them in the attic forever. Not if they're valuable. That's just crazy."

"Maybe you can come up with an idea for something to do with them."

"I don't know. Maybe we could give them to somebody to hold for us."

"Like who?"

"The museum, maybe. Do you think they do that?"

"Sure, why not? Or maybe you can suggest it. Instead of them buying them you can give them to them on loan."

"That's a good idea. That way the museum won't have to spend the cash to buy all this and the family can still officially own them."

When they got to Grace's house, no one was there. Tamika tried calling her mom's cell phone again, but still got no answer. "I guess we should just go home now."

"I'm sure she'll be in soon."

"I hope so," Tamika said, knowing better.

When they got back to the house, Sylvia was amazed by the transformation. "My goodness gracious, this place looks brand-new. When did all this happen? Did you do all this?"

"Mom supplied the credit card and I did the rest."

"You did an incredible job," Sylvia said after seeing the rest of the house. "It's just amazing. I'm very proud of you."

"Thanks, Aunt Syl."

"Now what do we have to eat? I feel like ice cream."

Tamika's cell rang. It was the hospital.

chapter 22

Laura

FInally awake, she winced at the pain as she shifted to get more comfortable. It was impossible. Laura sighed heavily, still exhausted for being in the emergency room all night. She slept most of the morning and awoke by the sound of her cell phone ringing. She didn't pick up but she did check her eight messages. The text message was concise and just what she needed to start her morning or rather her late afternoon. She got dressed slowly, smiling as she remembered the night before. They had laughed like crazy.

Instead of breaking in, Judith had a key and instead of doing any mischief they just sat in the cafeteria, ate bagged lunches, jumped rope in the gym and played music and danced on the auditorium stage.

The only real drawback she had from the episode last night was Tamika's frightened reaction to it all. She'd lectured all the way home. She could still hear the conversation ringing in her ears.

"Breaking into a school. Have you lost your mind?" she'd

said as she helped her into the car after staying at the hospital with her the whole time. "Do you have any idea how scared I was when the hospital called me last night?"

Laura had half smiled at the reversal of roles.

"It's not funny, Mom," Tamika added, still livid as she got behind the wheel and drove them home. "I can't believe you did that. Do you have any idea how dangerous that was?"

"Oh, come on, Tamika. It was a prank. We ate bologna-and-cheese sandwiches, chocolate pudding, chips and drank ginger ale. We walked around the school and even erased and cleaned off some of the classroom boards."

"That's not the point."

"It was a prank, something to do," Laura said as they pulled up in front of the house.

"And you got hurt."

"It was an accident. I could have slipped and fallen anywhere."

"But you didn't. You had no business in there and you know it. If it had been me you would have grounded me for life."

"Yes, fine, I messed up. It was a stupid decision that got out of hand, no big deal," Laura said.

"No big deal," Tamika repeated, stunned by her lackadaisical attitude. "It was irresponsible and reckless."

"It's all right, it wasn't like we broke anything."

"Mom, you broke into the high school, you broke the law and then broke or rather sprained your wrist. Plus the doctor said that you have a mild concussion. How is that all right? There's no way you should have gotten away with it." She opened the front door.

"We didn't. We have to pay a fine."

"Not good enough. I'd be grounded, wouldn't I?"

"Fine, I'm grounded. I'll stay in tonight."

"Mom, you sprained your wrist. You don't have a choice. All I'm saying is that you have to think before you act. This could have been much worse."

"Yeah, okay, that's one drawback," Laura said.

"Only one drawback. Are you kidding? You could have fallen and broken your neck or even worse."

"Now you're just exaggerating."

"I am not exaggerating," she said, helping her to the bed. "If I'd done something like that you would have a fit. As a matter of fact, I got the same speech when I messed up the kitchen last year."

Laura exhaled. "You're right, I was furious. Having a party like that when we were out of the house was dangerous and stupid and so was this."

That was apparently the end of the reprimand since Tamika had taken the rest of the time to get her into bed and make sure that she'd taken her pain pills.

Laura looked down at the bandage wrapped around her wrist and the sling on her arm. The fall off the stage was an eye-opener. Maybe her days of youth were at long last over. She picked up the newspaper that had been left on the nightstand.

She skimmed the article. Apparently the police were more humored than angry since they hadn't actually broken any laws other than poor judgment. The whole event had become a lavish joke as it was even written up on the front page with a screaming headline, After-Hours Alumni Revisit the Good Old Days. Looked as though they were off the hook. Of course, it helped that Grace, the mayor's daughter, was with them and Judith was on the school board and Fran was the principal's sister.

Laura went downstairs to the laptop, where she overheard the conversation going on outside on the front porch.

"How's your mom feeling?" Sylvia asked.

"Better. I checked on her a few hours ago. She was still asleep. The doctor said that the pain pills would knock her out for a while."

"Good," Sylvia said. "Now would you please tell me what on earth she was doing at the high school in the middle of the night?"

"I have no idea. Hanging out, I guess."

"Well, she's gone too far."

"Yeah, I think she knows that now," Tamika said.

"Y'all talking about me?" Laura asked as she opened the screen door and stepped out on the porch. "Good morning, Aunt Syl. When did you get here?"

"Last night, and apparently none too soon. But you would have known that had you not jumped off the stage onto your wrist. And yes, I was talking about you. What the devil were you thinking? I thought I taught you better than that."

"Yes, I know, dumb. Tamika was kind enough to point that out to me repeatedly last night, or rather early this morning. I think my days of hanging out are over."

"Finally," Tamika said loudly.

"So, what do you think about the house, Aunt Syl?"

"I saw it last night. It looks phenomenal. Your grandparents would have been proud of you," she said to Tamika.

"Her mother's proud of her too."

"So, did you tell her yet?"

"No, not yet," Laura said.

"Tell who what?" Tamika asked.

Both Sylvia and Laura smiled.

"I think she's earned it."

"Definitely, I think she has too."

"What are y'all talking about? You sold the house?"

"Tamika, I can't sell this house. It doesn't belong to me. I'm just the custodian."

"Custodian? So who owns it? You, Aunt Sylvia?"

"Not me, I'm not a Fraser."

"Me?" Tamika asked as both her mother and her aunt smiled at her knowingly.

"You," Laura said. "Your grandmother gave it to you years ago on the condition that you had to want it and earn it. I think you did both this summer rather well."

"You're joking, right?" Tamika asked. Laura shook her head, smiling. Sylvia mimicked her actions. "I own a house for real?"

"For real," Laura said. "Do you want to sell it?"

"I get to decide?" she asked. Laura nodded. "Then no," she said, looking up at the newly painted eaves. "But what about the taxes and the rest of it? What am I supposed to do about that? You don't have a job anymore. That means no extra money."

"Oh, I think we can handle that. At least until you're making millions with your photographs."

"Yeah, right. Winning the camp contest and getting published might have helped that along the way, but no big deal. I can do it some other time."

"There are other options," Laura said, handing her a flash drive.

"Like what? What's this?"

"It's the first draft of an article I wrote. It's about a mother and daughter and a summer they spent in each other's shoes."

"You wrote an article for the newspaper?"

"No, I wrote it for a magazine. I also took the liberty of sending and suggesting that they might consider using some of your photos for the piece since it's about our recent experiences. They agreed. They love your photos."

"What? Are you kidding me? I'm gonna get published?"

"Looks like, yes," Laura said.

"Mom!" Tamika squealed and jumped into her arms. "I can't believe it. Wait until Lisa hears this. I'm gonna be published in a magazine. Oh my God, this is going to look too good in my portfolio. Thank you, thank you, thank you."

"You're very welcome," Laura said, giggling happily. "Go check it out."

Tamika charged into the house and inserted the flash drive into the USB slot. A few minutes later, seeing her photos, she screamed again.

Sylvia chuckled. "I think she likes it."

Laura smiled and nodded. "I think you're right."

"I'm published! I'm published!" Tamika screamed as she came running outside, blasting the screen door wide open. "For real, they're gonna buy my photos?"

"Looks like. The magazine accepted the article and the photos. As a matter of fact, they're talking about an ongoing series."

Tamika screamed again. "I can't believe this. I gotta call Lisa and Sean!" She went charging into the house again.

"Huh, looks like you have some more business to handle. I better give you some privacy," Sylvia said as she saw Keith walk up the path. Laura turned and waved.

"Hi."

"Hi," he said. "I heard about the wrist. Are you okay?"

"Yeah, just fine."

Keith looked up at the outside of the building. "Wow, the place looks great. Looks like I'm gonna have to pay a bit more than I anticipated. But that's okay. It's worth it to help a friend out. I have the initial papers here for you to sign. We can discuss price later," he said as he reached into his suit pocket and pulled out an envelope and pen.

"Yeah, about that, technically, I can't sell you the house."

"What do you mean? Why not?"

"Well, it's not mine. It belongs to my daughter, always did." Tamika came outside. "Tamika, you have an offer to buy your house."

"You gotta be kidding me?" Keith said.

"No, the house and land were bequeathed to Tamika."

"What does a teenager know about business?"

"Apparently a lot. Tell me, what exactly are you going to do with it, if she were to sell it to you?"

Keith smiled. "More than likely continue what was started. Refurbish it, maybe add some modern touches. Bring it back to the splendor it was with the needed conveniences."

"Funny, I heard that you basically buy houses to tear down and resell the land. As a matter of fact, rumor has it that you already sold this house."

"Where'd you hear that?" he asked. She didn't respond. "It's business, Laura, progress," he said, directing his response to her.

"Well, not today. I think that Georgia will be just fine with one less mall. What do you think, Tamika?"

"I totally agree."

"Big mistake," he said.

"Not at all. You tried to get it two years ago from my mother and here you are again. Am I right?"

"I won't dignify that with an answer," Keith said, glaring

at Tamika, knowing that she was the one who told her mother about his plans.

Laura smiled inwardly. "Goodbye, Keith."

He turned and left without another word.

"How did you get so smart?" Laura asked, turning to her daughter.

"I learned it from my mom," Tamika replied.

"Well, you want to know what I learned from my daughter?"

"What?"

"I learned to take a chance, to step out of my comfort zone, enjoy life and live a little bit, but not too much."

"Know what I learned?" Tamika began. "Taking responsibility is harder than I thought. I don't think I'm ready to be an adult just yet."

"Actually, I'd say you are exactly ready. Tamika, you stepped up and took the lead and did an incredible job. I am so proud of you."

"Ya think?"

"I know." She winced, then sighed heavily. "Okay, that's it, I'm tired of being sixteen again. It's too hard and it's exhausting. I guess being a mom doesn't mean holding on to your child so tight that you strangle her dreams. It means letting go and letting her fly and being there no matter what." Tamika nodded. Laura smiled. "You, sweetie, are so beautiful," she said as tears rimmed the corners of her eyes.

"Hair and all?" Tamika asked.

Laura laughed and nodded. "Oh yes, most definitely hair and all."

"Sorry about Keith," Tamika said, genuinely feeling bad. "I know it's hard losing a friend, even one who never was," she added, thinking about Justin too.

Laura smiled at her daughter. "But it's wonderful finding a daughter and a new friend." She opened her arms and Tamika tumbled into them. They stood on the porch hugging as the love they felt pulled them closer and closer.

"Now, that's what I call a welcome home."

Tamika and Laura turned to see Malcolm standing on the porch step smiling at them.

"Dad, you're here! You're back!" Tamika exclaimed.

"My two favorite ladies," he said happily.

"Malcolm, what are you doing here?" Laura asked.

Tamika released her mother, then slammed into her father, receiving a huge hug. "You'll never guess what happened," Tamika began.

"I was in the neighborhood," Malcolm answered Laura, looking into her eyes softly, "so I thought I'd stop by. What happened to your arm?" he asked, seeing the bandage and sling.

"It's a long story. I'll tell you later," Laura said.

"But are you okay?" Malcolm asked.

"Yeah, I think I'm gonna be just fine now."

"Dad, you'll never guess what Mom did."

"What?"

"She wrote an article about us and the magazine is gonna publish it along with my photos. Can you believe it?"

"Great, but what about the photo camp?" he asked. "I understand there's another session this fall. You could attend after school."

"Photo camp, who cares about that now? This is the for-real deal. I'm getting published. Oh, this is too cool. Do you think that they might consider using my photos on a regular basis? I hope so. I guess we can figure that out later," she said, then squealed again, "I still can't believe it."

"In the neighborhood, huh? All the way from Japan?" Laura said, finally getting a word in.

"Yeah, something like that," he answered.

"Actually a crazy old lady suggested that I, and I quote, "'get my tired workaholic behind off that island and come see about my girls.'"

"Aunt Sylvia," Laura and Tamika said, laughing.

"Yeah, exactly. So I thought that it was about time I paid a bit more attention to my family."

"But what about Japan, your boss, your job?"

"Japan will always be there. And the job, well, I'm pretty damn good at what I do. Trust me, they don't want to lose me," he said. She nodded, impressed. "If I get the promotion, fine. If not, that's fine too. Don't worry, our paycheck isn't going anywhere. But what I couldn't get is our vacation plans changed like I hoped. It looks like we have to cancel Martha's Vineyard this year."

"That's okay," Laura said.

"Yeah, don't worry about it, Dad," Tamika said.

"Good, but also—" he reached into his pocket and pulled out an envelope "—I stopped at home. Your friend Lisa was just leaving." He handed her the envelope.

Tamika's face saddened as she took the envelope.

"Sweetie, I'm sorry. Maybe you can go visit her sometime," Laura said.

"Actually, I was thinking the exact same thing," Malcolm said. "I spoke to her mother and father and they're okay with it. That's not a letter from your friend, that's an online flight itinerary. You can leave tomorrow, if you want to go."

"For real, to visit Lisa in California?" she asked.

Malcolm nodded. "That is, if it's okay with your mother too. You'd have to trust her out there without you."

Tamika looked at her mother. Laura smiled. She knew that her little girl had grown up so much over the past year and particularly the last two months. "Yes, it's okay with me. Have a great time and be safe."

Tamika squealed and hugged her mother and father. "I gotta call Lisa and Sean," she said, then ran into the house.

"Sean?"

Laura glanced at Malcolm standing there staring at her. "I'll tell you about that later too. That was a nice idea to give Tamika a ticket to see Lisa. Of course, we won't be seeing her the rest of the afternoon."

"That's okay," he said as they stood there like strangers. "I have some catching up to do with my wife."

"Oh, really?" Laura said.

He nodded. "We're gonna talk, I mean really talk, and I'm gonna listen. I don't want to lose you, Laura, ever. So I thought maybe you wouldn't mind me hanging around here for a while."

"I'd like that." Laura smiled and nodded happily. That's all she ever wanted to hear.

"Did I tell you that you look fantastic?"

"Thanks." They stood smiling at each other.

"Hi, Mrs. Fraser. I heard about your accident. Are you okay?"

Laura turned to see Sean walking up the path behind them. "Hi, Sean. Yes, just fine."

He nodded. "Is Tamika around? I wanted to say goodbye since I have to go back to Boston tomorrow."

"Sure. Malcolm, this is Sean Edwards, a friend of Tamika's from Boston. He has family in Elwood, so he's been down for a few weeks."

"Hello, Mr. Fraser, nice to meet you, sir," he said as he

held his hand out to shake. The two stayed out on the porch talking while Laura went in to get Tamika.

"Tamika..."

"I called Lisa. She already knew that I was coming to visit. She's excited too. She's gonna call me back 'cause her and her mother are going out right now. I tried to call Sean too but I guess he went back already. He didn't say bye."

"I got a call from an Edna Hayes this morning. She left a message on my cell."

"Right, I was gonna tell you about her. She works at the Elwood Antique Shop and I took some things in to show her—pictures and some things from Joseph Fraser mainly."

"And..."

"She wants to make an offer to buy them."

Laura looked disappointed. "They belong to the estate, so technically they're yours to sell. So what are you gonna do?"

"Not sell them, first of all. And I was thinking since the museum burned down and they need exhibits that maybe we'd lend them some things. That way we still keep ownership and we know that it's in a safe place."

"I think that's a great idea." Laura smiled happily. "You know what, Tamika? I'm really, really proud of you," she said.

"You know what, Mom? I'm really, really proud of you too," Tamika said right back.

Dear Reader,

Jennifer and I hope that you enjoyed reading *She Said, She Said* as much as we enjoyed writing it. This was a very different experience for us—one I'm sure we will treasure for many years to come. As mother and daughter we had to depart from our traditional roles and develop a new common ground. As writers we had to learn to respect and accept each other's talents and limitations. The outcome was a wonderful story about stepping into another person's shoes and experiencing life from a different point of view and ultimately finding understanding and acceptance in others and in ourselves.

To help with this story Jennifer and I actually went on a road trip together and a lot of what happened in the book actually did happen to us. We laughed and joked and talked and cried. Yes, we even argued a bit. Throughout the course of writing this story we learned a lot about ourselves and each other. I think it brought us closer together in under-standing and love.

Best wishes,
Jennifer Norfleet & Celeste O. Norfleet

KIMANI
tru
™

Sometimes the right person
is closer than you think.

Monica McKayhan

indigo summer

Fifteen-year-old Indigo Summer's world finally
seems to be going in the right direction. The star
of the school basketball team has asked her out,
and she makes the high school dance squad all in
one week. But when her perfect world suddenly falls
apart, Indigo finds herself turning to her best friend,
Marcus Carter. The problem is now that Indigo
realizes what a great guy Marcus really is,
so does someone else.

"An engaging and compelling read."
—*Romantic Times BOOKreviews*
on *From Here to Forever*

Available the first week of February, wherever books are sold.

KIMANI
tru
™

She's got attitude…

Keysha's Drama

Bestselling author
Earl Sewell

When sixteen-year-old Keysha Kendall is sent to live
with the father she never knew, she finds herself in a
fancy house in middle-class suburbia. But Keysha
can't forget where she came from and she won't
let anyone else forget either. So she hooks up with a
rough crowd and does whatever she wants…
until what she wants changes real fast….

**"Earl Sewell has a knack for creating memorable
characters and scenes in his novels that stay with the
reader long after they've read the last page."
—*Rawsistaz Reviewers***

*Coming the first week of May
wherever books are sold.*